FL.

All her life Dana had felt isolated from
'normal' people and, despite the kind-
ness of those nearest to her, had
become almost a social outcast. Until
David arrived. He genuinely understood her agony, but then even he
rejected her . . .

FLASHBACK

BY

AMANDA CARPENTER

MILLS & BOON LIMITED
15–16 BROOK'S MEWS
LONDON W1A 1DR

First published 1984
Australian copyright 1984
Philippine copyright 1984
This edition 1984

© Amanda Carpenter 1984

ISBN 0 263 74836 7

Set in Monophoto Plantin 10 on 11½ pt.
01–1184 – 52203

Made and printed in Great Britain by Richard Clay (The Chaucer Press) Ltd, Bungay, Suffolk

To the humane amidst the humans who consider life to be a precious thing, and are concerned with the preservation of it. Maybe one day there will be no more war.

CHAPTER ONE

THE keen blade of the knife entered her midsection with a clarity of movement and efficiency that left her coughing with incredulous surprise and pain. The heat of the day pounded into her skin and her shirt stuck to her back. Now her shirt was sticking to her front as well, and her eyes looked a mute accusation at the wiry, foreign looking man that crouched menacingly in front of her. He looked so odd, but then so did the rest of the countryside, all green and brown and strange, as her blank, uncomprehending gaze slowly passed over it all. Then, just as slowly, she started to topple forward to collapse in a crumpled heap on the ground.

Her hand went to her stomach, groping, bunched into a tight, huge fist, which she stuffed into the wound with a grunt of pain to keep from bleeding to death right then and there. Dark red liquid oozed all over, on her hand, on the ground in front of her, and a trickle of salty sweat ran down the side of her face as half was pressed into the dirt. Pain, rage, despair. The incredible, strong will to survive. She would survive.

Then rough hands were flipping her over and yanking her hand away to determine the extent of the damage done, and she started to go hazy around the edges of her consciousness, jerking rigid at a sharp sting of fire-like pain. And then the cloudiness around the periphery of her vision started to darken, and the whole world blacked out into a monstrous nothing.

And the nothingness was part of the dream, and she couldn't wake up, or escape from it. She drifted a while, in a fog of pain.

Dana woke then, finally, her chest heaving in great, gasping sobs, sweat dampening herself and the sheet pulled over her slim, shivering body. A slight breeze moved a curtain at the open window, stirring her hair slightly. With the sickness of the horrible nightmare still gripping her, she took a shuddering breath, passed her hands over her eyes, and sat up.

The middle of the night, the blackest and most terrible time of all, when nightmares are real, even though they're insane, and despair is so hard to shake. The despair was gripping her now, and it was in its own way worse than the nightmare for it was reality, simple, unescapable. She moved like an old woman to the light switch on the wall and flipped it on with shaking fingers. Then, jerking up her nightshirt hastily, she stared down at her stomach with a half hopeful, half horrified look in her dark brown eyes.

The creamy skin was unmarred by any mark whatsoever.

She stood up, still with that strange, stiff movement that bespoke of an immense old age, and she started for the stairs at the end of the hall. If only she could get out of this head of hers and never have to worry about anything ever again! If only she knew for sure that she wasn't going totally, irrevocably, bizarrely insane . . .

'Dana?' her mother's sleepy, worried voice wafted down the hall to her. 'Sweetheart, are you all right?' A feeling of weary worry reached Dana, who knew that it was from her mother. She paused at the head of the stairs, unwilling to say anything, and her mother sighed through the open door, 'It was another nightmare, wasn't it, darling?'

'Yes, Mom,' she said raggedly. Two great tears spilled down her cheeks. 'Don't worry, I'm all right. I'm just going to read for a while downstairs, since I'm not very sleepy. You go on back to sleep.'

Something moving in the night air. Wind sighing. Silence, a distant creaking of bedsprings. Then her mother's weary voice again, wafting like the night breeze to the slim figure hovering indecisively. 'All right, dear. Though I wish you'd go to see Doctor Freedman and get some sleeping pills. This insomnia is going to push you to a collapse, if you aren't careful . . .' Her words trailed off, and Dana headed on down the stairs. She knew her mother wasn't going to say anymore. She'd known what her mother was going to say before she'd said it.

The house was much too hot and stifling. She crept upstairs to dress in jeans, a thin summer top, and sneakers, pulling back her chestnut hair and tying it with a ribbon, for comfort. Minutes later she was slipping out through the back door, needing desperately a chance to breathe fresh, cool air. There was no possibility of that, though, for outside it was as hot and as muggy as the house had been. The night sky was clear, the darkness clean and cutting to the senses, the dark purple sky awash with brilliant white flashing stars. There was no moon. The huge pines to the right of the house moaned and sighed as they bent first one way and then another in the restless wind. Dana walked listlessly, her feet automatically finding her way, knowing the area so well. But no matter how far she went she could never run from the nightmare that was herself.

She'd always tenaciously clung to the fact that she was, though definitely strange, undeniably sane down inside and fundamentally sound. But now, after the past several nights when she'd dreamt of a life she'd never even lived, she was becoming frighteningly convinced that she was going mad.

She was utterly terrified. This was something dark and new, something totally outside the realm of her experience. As a young girl, her parents had gradually come to the realization that she was something special, something extraordinary. It began when they had noticed that whenever someone close to her had been hurt, she would cry silently, tears rolling down her small face, and she would cradle the part of her body that had been injured on the other person. She didn't have to be told of the other person's injury. She never had to be told. She always knew.

When asked about it, she never could adequately describe in words what it was that she really experienced. In fact as she grew older, she had been simply astounded to find out that other people had no experience of that which she had taken for granted as a simple part of life. She could not believe that other people couldn't hear the unspoken messages that were fairly screamed at her.

As her parents had become more and more aware of Dana's peculiar talent: watching her respond to commands that were never uttered, wincing with a parent's pain at the shaking puddle of nervous hysteria that was Dana who had come home early from her first day of school, they'd decided to do their best to shelter her. They'd taken her out of the public school system and her mother, a qualified teacher, had retired early to teach Dana herself. No mention of oddity or strangeness had ever been allowed to reach her young ears, but then again, she knew what was being thought.

Now, in the darkness of the cloaking night, she had to smile a little at her parents' unquestioning support. They could have so easily looked at her as if she was a monster or a freak. But all she had ever received from them was that constant flow of their love and steady support.

As she'd grown older, she had done a little research and had finally labelled herself as a telepath. Picking up only certain people's emotions and thoughts and not others, never able to control it, never able to transmit her own thoughts and feelings, she had retired more and more into herself. She was always a loner, always shying away from personal contact like a frightened rabbit. She walked now through the iron veil of darkness, quietly crying. No matter how she had tried, she'd never found a way to shield herself from other people. She always picked up their emotions and upheavals like radar, with an unerring sense, and it was sometimes enough to make her scream with anger and frustration at her utter lack of privacy. Though she was only twenty, she felt like she'd lived forever.

She'd always held on to that feeling of reality, though. She'd always been able to trace her feelings to something that made sense. Mrs Reardon's fearful spurts of intense rage that Dana had sensed, her mind feeling scorched as if from a fiery blast, had been caused because she'd known her husband was cheating on her with the girl who worked at the post office.

That screaming, horrifying wrench of death that had hit her, three years ago, had been her father, smashed out of life almost instantly in an accident at the mill where he worked. It still made her break out in a cold sweat to remember that. When the message had come from sympathetic neighbours that Jerry Haslow had been killed, she had been rocking in silent grief beside her stunned and stricken mother.

But these queer, frightening nightmares made no sense whatsoever. She'd tried and tried, and she couldn't make any kind of continuity mesh between them and the world as she knew it. They were coming from no one she knew. She was completely, despondently alone in the madness.

The wind howled overhead. The night rustled, whispering softly to itself. Her head lifted, blindly seeking. She wasn't quite so alone. She found her voice and spoke out, 'Hello? Who's there?'

No answer. Pine rustle. The silent sound of stars twinkling. The wind caught at the grass and made it ripple, unseen. There was someone, a large black shadow that was the huge tree's shadow and not part of it, unmoving. She said abruptly, feeling alarmed, 'I know you're there, so there's no use in hiding. Who is it?' Her voice echoed queerly in the open space.

A low, masculine voice came back to her, slightly harsh, hostile. 'You're trespassing, whoever you are. For God's sake, it's four in the morning and hardly the time to be walking blithely about!' The black shadow moved, materialised into the shape of a man. He came nearer.

She felt that hostility like a silent snarl, and she reacted confusedly, backing up a few steps. 'H-hello, you must be the fellow renting the Cessler house, M-Mr Raymond. I'm your neighbour, Dana Haslow. I walk over the property quite a bit. Mrs Cessler never minds.' Her mind was working on several levels. She'd spoken almost absently, barely paying attention, for she was inwardly wondering if one day she might become dangerous to other people if she really was insane. Would she be able to hide it, or would she have to be committed? Could she cover up this great appalling rent in her personality? She wondered irrelevantly whether the food was good in a mental institution, and also why in the world this strange man was out of bed and abroad at four in the morning.

He had apparently come to the same conclusion, for after an obvious hesitation, that shadow that was a man came yet closer and said, dryly, 'It's—er—a bit late for wandering safely in the woods don't you think, Miss Haslow? If you were injured in an accident, it would be some time before anyone could find you.'

'I know the area well,' she said shortly. 'There would be no accident.' The whispering passage of a night owl overhead, and a sudden distant scream from a field mouse. She backed up again. He was sounding more friendly and at ease, but she still felt that hostility beat at her temples, and it alarmed her more than she cared to admit.

'Oh, but there might have easily been an accident just now,' he said pleasantly, and her throat tightened. He took a few more steps. He was too close. 'You see, as I didn't know your identity in the dark, I could have very easily hurt you, thinking that you were perhaps an intruder, maybe a thief come to break into the house——'

'Come off it, Mr Raymond,' she said, tension making her terse, and uncaring that she was so. 'This is such a small place that we don't even lock our doors at night. You're just trying to get me off this land, aren't you? But Mrs Cessler told me specifically that she was going to make sure you knew of me and that I was to be able to roam the property at will. You won't get rid of me so easily.' She didn't care what this person thought of her, knowing full well that she was considered to be a bit odd by just about everyone in the small town. Such a young girl keeping so stubbornly off to herself was bound to make someone talk. If they knew only the half of it, she thought.

'Not bad, for four in the morning. As a matter of fact, she did mention to me in passing that you had a habit of wandering around and that I should be lenient, as you'd done so all your life.' That male voice was fully mature and would be quite attractive, she thought idly, if it didn't have that thread of mockery running through it. He moved, became even more well defined. He was big. He must be just over six feet tall, she mused, but there was a solidity to the bulk that gave her an impression of a brick wall. The hostility had lessened somewhat, but there was a certain quality of tenseness about him that made her want to squirm. He was radiating as much nervous tension as she'd felt from the beginning, and the combination of both his emotions and her own had her nearly out of her head with the need to do something. She shifted, like a skittish colt. 'Tell me, Miss Haslow, are you in the habit of wandering around in the dead of night?' She sensed his sharp curiosity underneath the casual sounding words.

'I have insomnia,' she replied briefly, 'and am in the
habit of roaming around all over the place, whenever
the mood strikes me.'

'With no regard to your own safety, I see.'

She replied wearily this time, 'It's my life, or death, as
the case may be, and surely not your concern? I'll be off
the property shortly, as I am just crossing to the other
side.' She made a move as if to pass him on the path. He
remained immovable. She stopped impatiently.

'Hmn, also rude at four in the morning,' his voice
said, oddly amused. 'Grace told me that you were
extremely reserved, but she didn't mention the
rudeness.'

'Rudeness is a matter of perspective,' she murmured
calmly, though her whole being churned inside. Why
wouldn't he just get out of the way and let her go past?
She needed to run, to let out some of this volatile
emotion, to try to get exhausted. 'When one is polite,
one generally wishes for people to treat oneself with
that same politeness, hoping for friendliness in a
universally starved way that humans have, along with
a constant need for support and approval. I do not
have those kind of expectations, aspirations or
inclinations, and therefore I do not especially care if I
am rude or not.' She turned as she'd given up getting
past him and halted as if jerked by a puppet string at
the sound of his laugh.

'Such big words!' he mocked. 'I wonder if you know
what all of them really mean, and if you really mean
what all of them say?'

Not bothering to reply, she started again down the
path that took her back to the small, silent house and
went quietly inside to the darkness.

Finding her way on the ground floor, she went into the living room at the front of the house and groped her way to an armchair, which she sank into, sighing. The rest of the night, she knew from past experience, would be sleepless. She had no one to share her fears with, no one to share a madness that was mad even to her.

Her mother was a good, kind person. But she'd had her share of troubles lately and couldn't be expected to shoulder the burden of Dana's problems forever. She'd done so much for most of Dana's younger life, and it was time that she had the chance to do what *she* wanted to for a change. Just because her daughter felt emotionally crippled didn't mean that it should cripple her, too.

Dana stared into the blinding darkness. She was glad that her mother had got a teaching position for the fall and would be starting back to work. Now with her father gone and herself much older, her mother needed outside stimulation and her own interests. There was enough money from her father's life insurance, left to them jointly, to insure that neither would have to work again. They weren't rich, but there was enough money to pay the bills since the house and the land were owned outright. This was done with Dana in mind, and she knew and was grateful. But her mother needed a purpose.

Her mother was troubled by the nightmares. She never said, but of course Dana knew. She wished that she could ease her mother's fears, but she couldn't even ease her own. She felt so helpless.

God, she didn't know how to handle it.

Dana looked up as her mother came down the stairs

that morning. She smiled thinly. 'Good morning, Mom. Can I fix you breakfast?'

Denise looked at her daughter sharply, noting the purple shadows under her eyes and the grey shade of exhaustion colouring her face. 'No,' she said gently. 'I'll fix breakfast this morning. What do you want— bacon and eggs?'

Dana shook her head slightly. 'No, thanks. I think I'll just have juice and toast today. Besides, there are only two eggs left in the refrigerator. I was planning on walking to the store this afternoon.' She stood and followed her mother into the kitchen. 'I'm sorry I woke you last night.'

Another quick glance from her mother. 'That's all right, dear. No sleep again?'

Dana said shortly, 'No. But I'm not really worrying about it.' Blatant lie. She was amazed that her mother couldn't feel the lie from her, because she knew that she was transmitting it like a live radio. 'It'll go away when it's ready to go away and not before. I expect that will be soon though since the nightmares are fading already. The one last night was less clear and less intense. In fact I can barely remember it, now.' Another blatant lie, but her mother seemed to be well relieved because of it, and so she felt well justified for telling it.

Later on she walked to the grocery store, a short distance that gave her plenty of exercise and a chance to get out into the mellow sunshine. The wind was still howling, rustling trees and swaying bushes, and the warmth from the sun pulsed down on her bare head, making her lethargic and sleepy. She bought a few items, enough to fill their refrigerator with a few essentials but not too much for easy carrying. She was well known at the store for she went in all the time, and the shopkeeper's wife, Mrs Simms, chattered to her determinedly until Dana managed to slip away. Once outside she turned to walk back along the sidewalk and came up hard against a lithe, hard body. Sunlight glittered a moment in her eyes, bright and dangerous, and then she realised that she was looking into the hard, reckless eyes of a young man named Mick, who lived down the street from her and had just graduated from high school. His daredevil attitude and insolent behaviour had repelled her more than once before and now, as his hands came out to her arms automatically and touched her skin, she realised with a jolt just how close he was to that fine edge of danger. It was in his bored, frustrated eyes, and the hard, hurting grip of his fingers. She shivered as if she had a chill. The burning sun lit on dust motes that were dancing crazily in the air.

'Excuse me,' she said stiffly, trying to back away from him and get away from his touch. His hands tightened even more on her arms, though, and for the moment she was trapped. She hissed with pain.

'Well, well,' Mick drawled, looking her up and down consideringly, insolently. 'What have we here? Little Miss Snobbishness, isn't it? The one who always keeps to herself as if she's too good for anyone else. What's happening, little lady, or are you too stuck up to answer me to my face?'

'You always did have foul manners Mick, and I can see that you haven't changed,' she said coldly, looking at his hands with a sardonic raised eyebrow. 'Excuse me. I have a lot to do and you're obviously blocking my way.'

'Now, now, now,' he chided mockingly, his hands sliding higher to cup the soft flesh of her upper arms. 'Is that any way to be neighbourly?' His hands tightened. She would have bruises later. 'Surely even you can be nicer than that. Come on, show me how nice you can be, hmn?'

'Let go of my arms you bug, or I'll drop this five pound can of coffee on your foot,' she said, between her teeth, furious at how he was toying with her. He paused deliberately, laughing down at her tight expression, but there must have been some kind of hint in her eyes at how close she was to the edge of her control, for he then stepped back out of her way. He bowed her on past with that same insolent, mocking grin. She just looked at him contemptuously, refusing to show how she'd been shaken, and without another look or word walked right on by.

She walked on briskly back to the house, smiling occasionally at the different children that shouted and ran around with the wild abandonment that summer vacation invariably brought about. She had just reached the rather long sidewalk to the house when something impelled her to turn around slowly and look behind her.

A man was standing there some distance away, just watching her, still. She was far enough away so that she should not have been able to see his features very distinctly, but somehow she could. Brown hair, left long at the neck and short on his forehead, fluttered in the breeze and blew across his face. He looked to be in his thirties or thereabouts, and his face was distinguished by two lines running from nose to mouth, carved deeply. Another strong clean line between his brows, sensual lips, and dark eyes completed the face, and she then knew that she was seeing him with her mind and not her eyes. She just stared at him as he stared at her. Then she deliberately turned away and walked quickly to the house.

So that was their new neighbour, Mr Raymond, she mused. She'd known almost immediately who he was, and was in fact a bit surprised that if she was that sensitive to him, then why hadn't she seen him more clearly last night? But then she had been a bit distraught last night, and preoccupied. The vestiges of the nightmare had clung to her mind like an old spiderweb, and she hadn't been thinking clearly.

Once inside she quickly, neatly put away the things she'd bought and then, restless and needing some solitude, she ran lightly up the stairs to her room and retrieved her drawing pad and pencils. She would do some sketching today. Her fingers were itching to put something down on paper.

She called out to her mother as she went out of the back door and then looked around indecisively for a moment. She decided that she would trek over to a favourite resting place of hers. The movement and the solitude, as she headed for the path that would take her towards Mrs Cessler's property, helped to ease the tight band of tension that had been holding her in a muscle clenching clamp for the past few days. She was striding through dark blue shadow and bright yellow patches of scattered sunlight as great pine trees loomed overhead. Brown pine needles cushioned the path and covered the ground all around, with lacy light green ferns sprouting in the protecting shade. She wasn't paying attention to the lush, familiar scenery. She was engrossed in her thoughts, harking back to her ever-present fears, being haunted by that part of herself that set her apart from everyone else.

The ground angled up, the path leading to higher ground, and she was breathing slightly heavier as she finally broke from the trees and came out in a little clearing that jutted out into a crumbling, rocky cliff that plummeted a good forty feet to uneven, unyielding granite. There were even more pines growing down below. The clearing at the top of the cliff was a good twenty feet in a rough diameter, fairly well secluded and providing an excellent view of the surrounding land. With the attitude of one intimately familiar with both the view and the clearing itself, she threw herself down on the ground underneath a monstrously huge pine, and she propped herself against its trunk while she gazed out over the entire scene, sighing.

Loneliness. This place was so utterly lonely. She liked it. Nobody ever came this way, situated as it was on the border of their land and the Cessler property. And it was usually a good place to find some sort of peace and relaxation, secluded as it was. But for some reason today peace eluded her. She was too keyed up. Her restless fingers moved, opening her drawing pad to a blank sheet, and her nimble hands picked up a pencil, moving over the page, stroking efficient, quick lines over the white. Her eyes roamed over the view and then clouded over dreamily. She let her mind go free.

Footsteps on the path. She turned her head sharply at the sound, her concentration broken, her newly attained solitude abruptly shattered. Feeling invaded, she tensed and gritted her teeth, deciding determinedly to stay. Her eyes were stony now and no longer dreaming and soft. She turned back to the view, fingers tight against her pad of paper and her pencil. It snapped and she started with surprise.

The footsteps sounded closer, and then they stopped close by her. She said without looking around, 'Mr Raymond. Good afternoon.'

A pause. A bird up in her pine tree chittered noisily. 'Good afternoon, Miss Haslow,' he then replied, voice deep, expressionless. 'So this is a favourite haunt of yours?'

'Yes.' Her hands fell to her lap and lay idle. Should she get up and leave after all? The sun was shining but she sensed a darkness in this man that had nothing to do with the day. Her legs tensed, as if she were about to run a race. 'If you would like, I'll keep away after this. I don't mean to intrude.'

Another pause, and she heard him move. 'A generous offer, coming from someone who has roamed this land for years, and quite a change in attitude from last night. No, don't bother to get up. I don't feel I have the right to order you off the property and it wouldn't be kind if I did.'

Her hands trembled. 'Thank you.' Something was quivering in the air right in front of her, something intangible and ethereal and yet something so real that she would have staked her life on its existence. She sensed that, even as he was speaking to her courteously, his mind was on something entirely different, a vital thing, not having to do with her. His mind was clamped on that something with the tenacity and desperation of a fighting dog. For the first time since he'd joined her, she looked up. 'I apologise for my lack of manners last night. I was tired and on edge.'

'Insomnia does that to a person, I know. Please don't apologise. As I recall, I was not too bright or cheerful, myself.' He was staring out over the view, his dark head lifted to the breeze as if he were seeking something. The wind gently stirred his hair. She felt rather than saw his sigh and knew that he was relaxing slightly. It enabled her to unclasp her hands, and the tight band around her chest eased also. It was then she realised that it wasn't her own tension she was feeling, but his.

Crouching at his feet like she was and staring up at him, she saw how the line of power from the slim curve of his hips to the broader, solid curve of his shoulders was emphasised. She wondered how strong he really was. His head tilted and he considered her briefly, the sun putting his face into shadow and lighting the edges of his hair, and then he sat down beside her, draping his hands to dangle them carelessly from his raised knees. She suddenly wanted nothing more than to escape, but felt unable to get up and leave just yet. She jerked her head around to stare back out over the land. A large black bird soared overhead. She thought that it was perhaps a hawk, but wasn't familiar enough to identify the kind.

He was regarding her upturned face. 'My first name is David. Yours is Dana, if I remember rightly.' He paused and she nodded silently. Then he continued politely and all the while she knew he was just making sounds. She wondered what devil was plaguing him. 'Are you home from school for the summer?'

'No.' It had come out very short. His eyes

sharpened on her. She qualified what she had said and
softened the terse reply by saying, 'I'm not in college.'

'So. What do you do, then?' he continued. She
wanted to scream at him suddenly. The whole
conversation was such a farce, the sounds they were
mouthing so meaningless, his interest so false. She
could feel just how little he was really interested in
her, how she didn't matter at all to him. That wasn't
any concern of hers, she thought, straightening her
shoulders. She'd always dealt with the harshness of
uncompromising truth before. She certainly wouldn't
break under the truth now. She didn't care about him
any more than he cared about her.

She toyed with the broken pieces of her pencils,
fitting the jagged edges of the break together and
pulling it apart again. 'Nothing of importance. I don't
work. What do you do for a living?'

'I'm a writer. I do free lance work, mostly.' She
nodded without interest. She felt his gaze sharpen
even more on her and realised that his regard was fully
on her now. His interest had quickened. He'd felt her
uninterest in him almost as strongly as she'd sensed
his for her, and it intrigued him enough to catch his
attention.

She asked randomly, 'And are you working now,
Mr Raymond, or are you on vacation?'

'Call me David, if you like. I suppose that you could
say I'm on vacation. I'm taking a sabbatical from
work. I've been ill and this is a chance to rest
up before getting back into the swing of things.'
The blue jay that nested in the huge pine shot past
with the recklessness of a dive bomber and then
landed in a flurry on a low branch nearby, scolding

the bird that was too close to his nest.

That's a lie, she thought, and for one heart stopping moment feared that she'd said it aloud. It was a lie, but it wasn't any business of hers, and she didn't want to get into an awkward situation with this man, a total stranger. It was time she was leaving. She stood and, having forgotten her drawing pad, saw it fall on to the carpet of pine needles, pages fluttering. As she bent to retrieve it, she was just that split second too late as he reached forward automatically to pick it up for her. His brown fingers smoothed the pages back into place as she murmured a thanks, and he glanced at it idly before handing it back to her. He went absolutely, rigidly still.

His eyes were riveted on her unfinished drawing, and she felt the shock ripple through him like waves in a pond after a rock has been thrown in, felt it as surely as if it had been her, with the thudding at her own chest and temples. He went totally white, his knuckles tightening on the pad and ruining it. She flexed her fingers painfully. After the first overwhelming wave of shock that had rippled through him, she felt a nameless fear, but this wasn't coming from him. This was all her own, and she backed up a few steps, eyes huge.

'Where have you seen this?' The question came out of him with the force of a bullet. She flinched violently.

'I was just doodling,' she mumbled, shaking. What was wrong with him? What had upset him so?

'This isn't the view out there!' he said, from the back of his throat like a snarl, thrusting the picture under her face. 'This isn't an idle sketch!' She looked at her own drawing and moaned aloud, feeling sickened. The landscape she had drawn while idly dreaming there in the sun was totally alien to her and strangely complete, down to detailed work on the foliage. It was like nothing she'd ever seen before. 'Where have you seen this?'

She shook her head numbly, nauseated. 'Nowhere. It's my imagination. I made it up.' It was said hopelessly as she backed away, hardly aware that she did so, frightened by the violence of emotion coming from him. The clearing was too isolated suddenly.

'You didn't make this up. How old are you?' He advanced on her.

'Twenty . . .' her voice wobbled.

'You're too young to have been there.' His own voice was hard, harsh, and she wondered, been where? 'Where have you seen this?'

'Nowhere! Nowhere, I swear it. Look, you can have the picture, I don't want it. I was just sketching, really.' She stared up at him, having gone white herself, and she saw the darkness in his eyes, the dilated pupils, the agressiveness to his rock-hard face, the pulse that beat rapidly, betrayingly at the base of his throat. She felt and saw how very dangerous he really was. It invaded her own blood stream and started her own heart to rattling away in her chest, pounding at her wrists and temples. She suddenly tripped backwards, sprawling at his feet. He reached down and hauled her up unsympathetically, his hand hurting where he gripped the spot that Mick had bruised, but she didn't notice the hurt because realisation was exploding inside of her like a bombshell, prompted by his physical touch. And the sickness grew in her as she realised that the picture was not from her mind but from his, and she covered her mouth with one shaking hand, muttering, 'Oh, God.' He was looking an angry inquiry, more like an accusation, and it was more than she could stand.

She twisted from his grasp and fled.

CHAPTER TWO

THE plane was landing, hitting the ground with a rough thump and rolling, and then everyone was shouting and grabbing their things and jumping down on to the ground as shells exploded by the runway. Everyone ran for a squat, oblong building that looked as if it had been pieced together with a few sheets of metal, some glue and a few prayers. Dana picked up her duffle bag and ran with the others. It was the heat that hit her the hardest. The heat, after coming from the relatively cool interior of the plane, was like a furnace blast right in the face. It caught at the blood, made the pulse beat like a warm drum in the temples, made one gasp like a beached fish.

The area looked alien, all greens and browns and strange vegetation, and it was all taken in that swift dash for the building. She entered with everyone else, and men, dressed in drab olive fatigues, shuffled into some semblance of order while an officer walked up and down in front of them.

A long, long time passed and the fellow droned on and on and on, and Dana's head started to ache with the heat and the alienation of everything, and the fatigue, and that man's endless talking. Then everything changed, and the officer was standing right in front of her, staring at her intimidatingly, but she looked him right in the eye, undaunted, expressionless.

He suddenly shouted, 'Do you believe in hell, lieutenant?'

'No, sir.' And her voice was deeper, rumbling, and it was at that moment that she knew that the dream was not her own but someone else's. And it was also then that she knew she was helpless to get out of the dream until whoever it was had finished dreaming it also. She was trapped.

The officer in front of her/him became leering, evil, his face changing into something horrible and horrifying. 'You will, boy. Believe me, you will. By this time next year you'll be wishing you were out of this place or dead, it won't matter which, as long as you're out of this place. 'Cause do you know where this is, boy? This is hell.' And it echoed in her mind weirdly until she thought she would scream. This is hell, is hell, ishellishellishell.

Dana bolted upright in her bed, rigid and sweating, crying and panting, and she crouched for some time in her bed, muscles quivering from reaction and weariness in the dark night. Then she slowly, achingly dragged herself out of bed after an incurious glance at her clock. It was only three thirty in the morning and she'd only slept around five hours, but she knew that there would be no more sleep—again—for her that night.

Grey shadows of exhaustion loomed in Dana's head that morning, as she pulled herself up the stairs to shower. The water she turned on was deliberately cold, and the shock of the icy spray jolted her into a painful wakefulness. She then sudsed quickly, soaped her hair and rinsed it, and then crept out of the shower cubicle, shaking and gasping. Her fingers were tinged with blue as they sorted through her clothes numbly, and she managed to shrug into her jeans and top, coldness making her clumsy. Then she took her hair dryer and worked diligently at getting the long strands of thick chestnut hair at least partially dry. It fell to past her shoulder blades, and she had to bend forward to let her hair fall over her face in order to dry it. Then she swung her head back and her hair settled with a swirl on to her shoulders, the weight of it familiar, not even noticed.

Her jeans were loose at the waist, and she grimaced at that, irritated. At the best of times she was slim, and with her lack of appetite lately her slimness had given way to a more angular thinness, her arms looking like fragile sticks and the elbow bone becoming pronounced. Her hips jutted out more prominently. She glanced at herself in the mirror and thought disgustedly that she looked like a store mannequin, lifeless except for a glitter of something in her grey-green eyes that looked a bit feverish, like something stretched tight. That nervous core of tension still was gripping her. The loss of weight hadn't done much for her face either. The hollows of her cheekbones seemed to her to be too pronounced, and her neck looked too slender to hold up the heavy weight of her head and thick, heavy fall of hair. No amount of weight loss could take away the fullness of her mouth or the rich quality to her glimmering, heavy lidded eyes, but other than those two positive points, she looked almost like a starved cat.

She would try to eat breakfast today, she decided, after a critical assessment of herself in the mirror. This was getting to be ridiculous.

But later on, when she was seated at the kitchen table and staring despondently down at her food, she found that she just couldn't force down the meal to her protesting stomach. And so her meal was thrown away, again.

She decided that morning that she would go to visit Mrs Cessler, the elderly lady who had for many years been their neighbour and who still owned the land and house which David Raymond was renting. Mrs Cessler had been a nice neighbour, living in a gentle, perpetual state of mild sadness, missing her dead husband and reliving her happier past. Dana was good friends with her, finding her sympathetic and kind, and more than willing to have a quiet, rather withdrawn visitor. Now the older lady could not live at home alone, because of an accident and a broken hip, and so she had rented her house recently to David Raymond and currently lived with her sister as her brittle old bones slowly and painfully healed.

Dana had been to see Mrs Cessler several times already, and one subject they never broached was just how Dana had known that the older lady had been hurt. Dana had been the one to find her, crouching in pain at the bottom of her stairs. She'd been afraid the first few times she'd gone, that Mrs Cessler would become curious about that and ask her uncomfortable questions, but the old lady said nothing and Dana gradually grew easier in her mind and relaxed.

After telling her mother where she was going, Dana left the house and headed for the garage which was a separate building from the house. She entered, opened the garage, and reversed the car competently. Mrs Cessler and her sister lived on the other side of town, and Dana forced herself to drive very carefully. After two weeks or so of very little or no sleep, she was wary of having an accident through sheer exhaustion. She pulled up by a tiny home that was nestled in a landscape of several neatly trimmed bushes, with two oak trees. She parked just behind a car in the street, in front of the house, and ran up the walk to tap lightly at the door. Footsteps sounded, heavier than she'd expected, and the door swung to reveal to her David Raymond. He stood still, staring frowningly down at her.

She backed up an involuntary step, muttering something; she wasn't sure what. Then he was swinging the door open wide and calling over his shoulder, 'It's Dana Haslow, Grace. Come on in, Dana.' And she heard the older lady call out a welcome from the living room. She had no choice. Even if she'd entertained a brief, vague hope of leaving and coming back later, she had to go in now.

Stepping gingerly by the silent and still man, she sent him an uncertain, wary look before heading on into the living room with as much of an appearance of normality as she could muster. Mrs Cessler was positioned on the couch where she spent all her day, still in a heavy cast. Dana noticed with a pang that her hair since the accident had become even more wispy and white, and her lined face seemed to have shrunken in under the eyes and in the hollows of her cheekbones. She had aged.

Dana went over and gently kissed her on her frail seeming cheek before finding the armchair by the couch to sit in. She avoided looking in David's direction, being painfully aware of his silent wariness and unspoken dislike. She was also overwhelmed in the simple awareness of pain, for Mrs Cessler always seemed to be suffering some discomfort. She determinedly ignored it as best she could. If the older lady could be silent and uncomplaining, then so could she. These visits were always very hard on Dana, but she knew how delighted Mrs Cessler was to see her and how much it meant to her. So she gritted her teeth and came anyway.

'Dana, my dear!' Mrs Cessler said brightly, settling back on to her pillows and smiling. 'It's always so good to see you. But you aren't looking well, child. You've lost so much weight! You and David, I can see, have much in common. Have you met David?'

'Yes, we've met,' she murmured, not quite understanding everything Mrs Cessler had said. She didn't glance his way and leaned forward in an effort to get control of the conversation. 'And how are you doing? You're looking better every time I see you.'

'Nonsense!' the older lady snorted, and a twinge from her still tender side made Dana wince. Her eyes caught David Raymond's quick glance, and then slid away. She tried not to think of what had happened the day before. She wondered what he thought of it, and her. She knew that he didn't trust her; this distrust came through as clearly as his dislike of her. She didn't really understand why, unless it had something to do with the strange picture she'd drawn and he had recognised. What had she drawn? Why would it make him react so violently? She focused on what the older lady was saying to her. '. . . and it's been such a comfort to know that he is taking care of my house instead of some stranger. I know that David will keep

things well taken care of.' And she smiled at him
fondly.

Dana nodded, unsurprised. 'I was wondering how
you'd managed to rent the house so soon after your
accident.' She addressed David personally. 'Are you
two related, then?'

As he nodded, still watching her from under
lowered, heavy brows, Mrs Cessler answered verbally,
'Yes, dear. He's my cousin's grandson. I don't believe
that you have met that side of my family.' Dana shook
her head.

After talking for a few more minutes, she then
sought the opportunity to leave, but Mrs Cessler
would have none of it. She listened, resigned, as the
older woman extolled her to stay and perhaps fix them
all some fresh coffee. After a few demurs, with David
in his corner staying absolutely silent, Dana finally
gave in when she saw that the other woman was just
not willing to let her go yet. And so, with a sinking
heart, she went into the kitchen to prepare a tray and
start the coffee maker.

As she was about to carry the tray into the other
room, a sound at the doorway made her jump and turn
around. David was of course there, lounging against
the doorpost and watching her unnervingly. She was
unsurprised. Even if he hadn't been the only mobile
person in the house, she would have felt his entrance
even as she heard his footsteps. After a wide-eyed
stare at his unfathomable expression, she turned and
with trembling hands rearranged the cups on the tray,
without speaking. The air was charged with things left
unsaid and questions she knew he wanted to ask her,
and that wary hostility.

He made a move and she just waited for him to say something, any of the things that were hovering on his lips, but all he said was, 'I came to see if I could help carry anything in for you. You don't look strong enough to carry a flea, let alone that heavy tray.' He came away from the doorpost and walked her way. His stride was lithe.

She backed away from the tray immediately as if it had become contaminated, using the opportunity to put distance between him and her. Why did he make her feel so edgy, so tense and stretched tight? Why was she so sensitive to this man, of all people? 'I'm stronger than I look,' she muttered, and he cocked a sardonic eyebrow at her.

'You'd have to be; you don't look strong enough to hold your head up straight. Grace is right. You're too thin.' He picked up the tray and then went on into the other room. She was left cocking her head in silent sarcasm to his back, suddenly, surprisingly, mirthfully grinning at his unprecedented personal remarks.

Back in the living room she poured, kneeling in front of the coffee table and handing a cup first to Mrs Cessler and then to David. She backed away from him immediately and felt a surge of irritation from him at this. So he'd noticed it before. She took her own cup and retreated back to her chair, sipping at it as an excuse to keep from having to say anything. The whole visit had rapidly become a fiasco for her. Nervous, uncomfortable, with Mrs Cessler's pain rubbing at her raw nerves, Dana felt close to the edge of something. She felt as if the tightness in her head was about to explode or break. She felt ready to lose all control, ready to fall into a pit and never climb out again. She felt—with a queer sense of shock in her heart, she felt that it was not her own crisis she felt approaching, but that of the strange man sitting across the room. It was David who was stretched so tightly something was bound to snap. It was David who was exercising such a rigid control over himself that the tightness and the desperation were reaching out and grabbing her by force. She was unable to shake it off; she was as caught as him.

Dana had fallen silent as her thoughts rattled through this revelation, and the other two were talking on, apparently not noticing anything wrong with her other than the fact that she had withdrawn moment-arily from the conversation. With a sluggish click back to the surface, she focused only partially on what was being said, still with half of her mind on the undercurrents in the room and her own surmises.

'. . . and weren't you doing something else about six years ago?' Mrs Cessler was asking David. Dana heard the last of the question, but she didn't catch the context of it or the first part and so she wasn't sure what was being discussed. She glanced briefly at David and found him looking down at his hands as he lounged easily in his chair. 'I thought your grand-mother told me something about you working as an editor for a newspaper, right?'

She didn't know what came over her. She had only been paying attention with half her mind; she wasn't even planning to speak; she'd every intention of just sitting back and staying silent until she could somehow contrive to slip away without hurting Mrs Cessler's feelings. But Dana found herself saying offhandedly, 'Oh, that was four years ago, not six.'

And even as the words came out of her mouth she
tried to catch them back, to stop them from being
uttered, but they'd already flown out like a bird who
launches and hovers a moment in the air before
soaring.

Silence. Mrs Cessler and David looking at her
sharply. Her hand crept to her mouth and her eyes
widened, and she felt sickened at what she'd just done.
Where had that come from? Even if she'd sensed his
thoughts before he spoke them, she usually had
enough control over herself to hide that, to keep silent.
Just after her own wave of sickening shock came a
wave of fury so intense from him she thought she'd
physically been hit and blanched. It swamped her like
a tidal wave.

But all he did in actuality was let his features go
completely cold and mocking, letting his contempt and
dislike for her show without any attempt to mask it.
'Since Miss Haslow knows so much about me,' he said
with a softness that made her turn her head away,
'why don't we just let her answer all your questions,
Grace? She obviously has a good source of information.' His very quietness was biting enough to make
tears come to her eyes. She looked down at her hands
as they twisted together in her lap, her face stricken.

'I really don't know what came over me, I—I'm
sorry, I——' her muttered apology, spoken dully,
petered away into nothing and like a recalcitrant child
caught in a crime, she hung her head miserably.

His fury had not abated and that more than
anything lashed at her. 'You don't know what came
over you to listen to gossip, or you don't know what
made you give yourself away?' he asked, with that

quiet, intensely sarcastic voice. 'You really must tell me your source of information. They must be damned good to get such facts—perhaps I could learn a few tricks from them to help my journalistic endeavours.'

Face white, eyes sick, she looked to the older lady and found Mrs Cessler smiling at her with such compassion that it, more than anything, made two great tears splash down her cheeks. She stood abruptly, clattered her cup and saucer on to the tray without looking to see if it had landed safely, and mumbled, 'I'll be by to see you again soon.' And without looking at the still seated, furious man across the room and too near, she headed for the front door at a run.

He was quick to get out of his chair in a kind of lunge, and was after her even as she was opening the door and she could feel him coming, could feel his intent so that her fingers trembled in panic, and then she was out of the door and heading for her car blindly. She wouldn't make it. He was too fast.

Mrs Cessler called out sharply, 'David! Let her go, please!' Then more sharply, 'David, I must talk to you right now! Please, come back inside!'

He stopped at the doorway, one hand clenched on the doorpost, as he watched Dana climb into her car and drive away. The anger was still throbbing in him. It was so strong and overpowering that it began to frighten even him. He took a few deep breaths, chest heaving, in an effort to calm down. The edge was closer than he'd thought. It was right there beside him, and he'd have to be very careful to make sure he didn't lose all control. He clamped down on his emotions, asserting his own will over them until he found himself becoming calmer. Then, bit by bit, he forced all of those dangerous feelings out and locked them away. When he went back into the living room, scant moments later, his face was normal, expressionless. He sat down and looked at the old woman.

Grace Cessler was staring down at her gnarled, fragile hands. She plucked at the fringe of the afghan that covered her. Then she started to speak, strangely hesitant. 'I want to tell you something, David. I want to tell you something that, for young Dana's sake and for your sake, I don't want you to repeat to anyone. Not anyone, do you hear? Will you promise me that, my dear?'

Frowning now in puzzlement, he curtly made his promise, and without realising it leaned forward in his chair. She smiled at him and cleared her throat, as if self-conscious.

'I remember when the Haslows moved in right by me. They were such a handsome family. They were everything a family should be, warm and caring and full of laughter. They seemed ideal to everyone else. And I remember Dana. She was such a pretty little thing, all eyes and braids and as quiet as a church mouse. When autumn came around, she was to have gone to school as she was of age, along with the other children in the neighbourhood. But she didn't go and at first, when I thought about it, I'd assumed that her birthday had fallen just on the other side of the cut-off date for starting school. But I saw that it couldn't be so when she didn't go the next year either. Please bear with me,' she added, smiling, though he had made no impatient move. 'I have a point to make and I'm trying to get around to it in the right way.'

'I wasn't interrupting, Grace,' he said quietly, eyes slightly twinkling. Without being asked he reached forward and refilled her cup, and she thanked him.

'No, you weren't. You are a good boy, you've always been a good boy. It's just that I think I know how you are going to react to what I want to say. But never mind that now. I'll just go on and leave you to react how you will. Of course, all of this was happening over a period of years and, I must confess, I showed only a passing interest in what happened to little Dana, being involved as I was with grieving at Karl's death and wrapped up in my own affairs. But it was very noticeable that she was unusually secluded as a child, and I wondered why. She seemed perfectly normal to me. She did not have a physical handicap that I had noticed, and was not mentally retarded to the best of my knowledge. I remember one conversation that I had with her mother, Denise. Have you met her?'

He stirred himself and answered shortly, 'No. In fact, I barely know Dana, only in passing. She roams all over the place, just as you'd warned.'

Mrs Cessler smiled. 'Yes, she's a restless soul. But getting back to that conversation, I happened to ask Denise if Dana had a learning disability and was being kept out of public school because of that. I still remember the strange look she gave me. She just hesitated and then said, no, Dana was perfectly able to keep up and even surpass many youngsters her age. That was when I found out that Denise was a teacher and had left her career to teach Dana, herself. That's quite something, isn't it? Many people would have supplemented their child's learning with perhaps something on the side, but to actually leave a career to devote all that time to their child's learning development is something extraordinary. The Haslows weren't rich by any means. They did well enough on Jerry's salary, but they would have been much more comfortable if they'd had the added income from Denise's teaching. But it was still not something in itself that was so different that it caught my eye. No, what was different about little Dana was that she never played with other children who lived on the block. She seemed perfectly happy to play by herself in the house, or outside, and it even seemed to me that she avoided other children. It wasn't her parents. They acted very normally around her, and never seemed over-protective. No, it was Dana's own choice, so whenever I was around the child, I perhaps watched her more closely than I would have normally, because she'd caught my eye. And I noticed little things about her . I remember I was over having coffee with Denise, and Dana was colouring in a picture book on the floor beside me. This sticks out in my mind as clearly as if it had happened yesterday. It was the first time that I'd ever been over for any length of time at their house, and the first time, to the best of my knowledge, that I'd ever had coffee at the Haslows' in front of Dana. I take sugar in my coffee, and the sugar bowl had been out of my reach. Before I'd made any gesture towards the bowl, indeed, just as I'd framed the intention in my mind, Dana silently got up from the floor and handed the sugar bowl to me, just like that.'

His eyes, which had wandered to the carpet in front of him, returned sharply to her face. She could tell that for the first time since her narration had begun, his interest was snagged. He said slowly, 'So, she was an observant and intelligent child. Is that what you wanted to tell me so badly?'

Mrs Cessler slowly shook her head, her wispy white hair framing her lined face delicately. 'No. I'm only partially through with my story, David. After she handed the sugar bowl to me, Denise and Dana just looked at each other, as if they'd been caught in the middle of a guilty act. Then, without a verbal word from her mother, Dana went and picked up her crayons and book and left the room.' Grace stopped and then realised that she had braided the edge of the fringe together with her restless, wandering hands. She very carefully began to take it apart. Then with an apparent change of subject, she said, almost idly, 'Jerry Haslow died three years ago in an accident at the mill where he'd worked. It was—horrible. A few of the supervisors came by and asked me to help them tell Denise; I went over to their house, with another neighbour you haven't met yet, and we knocked on the front door for a long time. No one answered, so we went in after trying the door and finding it unlocked. We found Denise sitting on the couch beside Dana, looking stunned and grief-stricken, and Dana . . . well, Dana looked as if she'd been hit by a car. She couldn't talk to us. She was all huddled in a shaking ball and we couldn't get her to stop trembling. David, they already knew that Jerry was dead.'

Grace dared to look at him then, and she found him staring at her with an arrested look on his face. He was leaning forward, long fingered hands clasped, elbows resting on knees, and his intelligent, dark face intent. 'You're trying to tell me that Dana is somehow telepathic,' he said flatly, and the flatness was an automatic protestation of disbelief.

She hesitated. 'I think so. You see, there's one more thing I'd like to tell you, and I've never mentioned this to anyone before now, not even to Dana. When I fell down the stairs, all those months ago, I was all alone in the house. You know the position of the staircase. There is no way anyone could have seen me on the floor because there aren't any windows that show the area just at the foot of the stairs. I don't really remember how long I laid on the floor since I was in a lot of pain, but it couldn't have been more than five minutes when I heard glass breaking at my back door. I'd locked the door the evening before—I can remember that very vividly—it comes from having lived too long in the city, I think. A few moments later, Dana stumbled into the room. She was limping and holding her side.' Grace smiled and the smile held more than a hint of remembered pain along with a great deal of affection. 'I didn't put it together at the time, David, but I've had plenty of time to think since the accident, and to remember. Dana was limping and favouring her left leg, and it was my left hip that had been broken. She was holding her left side as if it hurt her, the side where I'd broken three ribs. And there is no way on earth that I know of that she could have known I'd hurt myself.'

Silence again in the room. David looked down at his hands and then at the carpet a while, and Grace waited patiently for some kind of reaction. Finally he looked at her, and there was a glimmer of a rueful smile in his dark eyes. 'I have to believe what you are saying since there are too many points in your story that can be

corroborated with other people. Still, it's quite
something to swallow all at once. One always hears of
this kind of thing happening—I guess you'd call it
psychic phenomena—but it's always easy to doubt
when there is no first hand experience. Do you have
any idea of how controlled she is with this ...
sensitivity?'

She shook her head. 'No. She never talks about it,
and can you blame her? Can you imagine the
reaction of some people, the risk of ridicule, or
worse, ostracisation? The child's had enough to bear
as it is. I wouldn't have told even you anything,
David, except that I didn't want you to blame her
for somehow "knowing" something about you that
she perhaps logically shouldn't have. She can't help
it. And I must say, I think you are taking this very
calmly, for just having heard it from a sick old
woman.'

He shook his head and clasped her hands
affectionately. 'Stop that, or I won't come back to visit
you, ever again. I have to admit that something had
already happened to make me wonder a bit—oh, it's
nothing, really. It was just something like today,
where she'd known something she by rights hadn't
any access to and could have had no previous
experience of . . .' His voice trailed off into nothing as
his dark eyes widened with some kind of shock and he
whitened visibly, muttering, 'Oh, my God.'

Grace leaned forward, alarmed. 'What is it, David?'

With an apparent effort he managed to shake off
whatever had hit him and he smiled at the worried
woman. He took in her tired face and realised that the
visit must have taken more out of her than she was

willing to admit. 'It's nothing, less than nothing. No, really, it was just a passing thought.'

Driving home, Dana was furious to find that her hands were visibly shaking; indeed, her whole body was trembling with reaction. With a wave of anger, she thought of how David Raymond had intimidated her, even before she'd made a fool of herself by butting into a conversation and exposing herself to so much criticism and—from his point of view—justified anger. And it was all because of some sketch that she'd made of an unknown place. What had she drawn, anyway? As she thought back, wondering, the realisation hit her with that same sickening dread that she'd felt when she heard herself speak, scant minutes before.

She had drawn the same alien landscape from her nightmares. That was where she'd seen it, where she'd got the idea. And the picture had meant something to David Raymond, something vitally important. She pulled into her driveway automatically, shifting down and then switching off the ignition. But the picture had been from his mind.

Obviously, then, the nightmares were, too. They had begun to make a queer sort of sense, even to her, who had no idea really of what was going on in them. They were connected enough in theme and form so that she guessed that they were actually nightmares from memory, not from the mind's imagination.

Not from her imagination, at any rate. She wasn't going crazy, at least not quite yet. She was merely dreaming David Raymond's dreams. 'Oh, my God,' she whispered, as the thought struck her.

And she wondered briefly, just before she opened the car door to get out, at how the phrase seemed to echo in the confines of the interior.

She slammed the car door behind her, still shaking, and cursing it. Why was she so out of control now? Realising that she was mentally involved with another person had never hit her so hard before. She was surely acquainted with her own self enough not to be shocked by what she was experiencing now. Why was she feeling this incredibly powerful jumble of emotions? Why was she shaking with anger and dread and a certain kind of violent fear she'd never known before?

Why did she feel so dangerous?

She burst into the house and slammed the door behind her, panting a little at her headlong rush into the house. She wiped at something that trickled down her forehead and realised how profusely she was sweating. The edge, she was at the very edge. Perhaps she was wrong after all. Perhaps she was going stark raving mad. Perhaps the pressure and the utter vulnerability of her self to others was finally getting to her, as she'd always known it would. Perhaps——

She turned shortly and stared at her mother, just now entering the living room. Something of her emotional upheaval must have shown in her face, for Denise said sharply, 'Dana? Are you all right? You look absolutely dreadful.'

She licked dry lips and said shortly, 'I'm fine.' She turned on her heel and headed for the kitchen, her movements jerky and uncoordinated. She needed a drink badly. Turning on the faucet at the kitchen sink, she stuck a finger under the gushing water until the flow became suddenly cold. Then she grabbed a glass, held it under the water flow, and switched off the faucet as she tilted the glass up to her mouth, drinking greedily. She didn't stop until the entire glassful had flowed down her parched throat and then filled it and drank again. It was so hot, hotter than any other summer she could remember. She set the glass down on the counter and slowly turned to face her mother, who had followed her into the kitchen. She could feel her mother's sharp worry.

Denise surveyed her for a while and then asked abruptly, 'How long has it been since you've had a decent meal inside you? Have you eaten at all today? Look at you—you're as thin as a stick.'

Dana clenched her hands, and felt the sweat on her palms. 'Don't nag at me,' she gritted, between her teeth. 'I'm all right. Can't you just leave me alone?'

A flicker of surprise on her mother's face, and then a look of anger. 'There is no call for being rude, young lady, no matter what you think the provocation. I won't have that tone of voice from you, do you hear? Now sit down and I'll fix you something to eat.'

'Didn't you just hear what I said?' Dana suddenly exploded into a shout. 'I said to leave me alone, for crying out loud! I don't want to eat—I'm all right. Just drop it, will you?' She turned away, feeling close to the end of her rope and nearly ready to break into tears. She was just so tired. She hadn't slept well in years, it seemed, and she stumbled from sheer exhaustion.

Even in the midst of her own emotion, she could feel her mother's reaction, the anger, the bewilderment, and the ever present worry that worked on

Dana's own patience like water on a stone. Even her own mother thought she was going loony. 'Dana, sit down! You look as if you're going to fall any moment now. I'm going to call the doctor and get you an appointment. You don't look well at all.'

'Why can't I *make you understand*?' Dana's voice rose to a scream, putting her two fists against the sides of her head as if a bell was pealing intolerably in her ears. 'Oh, I can feel you loud and clear, but every time I try to communicate *my* thoughts and *my* feelings to you, you don't even hear what I'm saying! I said to leave me alone! Get out of my head! You're all crowding me to death!'

She turned drunkenly as her mother stood there stunned, and she ran out of the kitchen and up the stairs. Rushing headlong into her bedroom, she locked the door behind her and threw herself on to her bed and spent all of her pent-up feelings in a storm of hard, racking, dry sobs. Images flashed by in her head of the terrible nightmares, the sweating fear, her own precarious control and finally, the unknown future. As she tried to look beyond that blackness, exhausted, futilely looking for some ray of hope, it overwhelmed her and sucked her right in.

She slept.

CHAPTER THREE

ABSOLUTELY nothing of importance happened to Dana for the next few days. The weekend came and went, the weather darkened to rain and blustery gusts of wind, and then became fair again on Sunday evening; both she and her mother studiously avoided one another, both still feeling a bit tender and self-conscious about their uncharacteristic clash; and Dana had not one single nightmare come to plague her night's repose.

She became physically rested again, ate a little more, and was generally able to present a more or less normal aspect for others' viewing.

Nevertheless, in spite of the innocuousness, the complete and utter normality of the passing days, the peacefulness of it all, Dana still felt stretched tight, on edge, starting at any undue noise or sudden sound. She would start awake in the middle of the night, looking around her wildly, checking out of her window to make sure everything was still sane and peaceful. She wasn't sure what she was watching for; all she knew was that she was worried and frightened. It was a perpetual fear, as if she expected to die any time, as if she expected the world to turn into an enemy, as if she expected someone to walk up and put a knife in her back. And as she thought of that, she remembered one of the nightmares that she'd had, of that cool, clean blade sliding so easily into her skin, right into her own stomach. In spite of her intellectual knowledge of her unmarked skin, the feeling was so vivid in her mind and the remembrance of the nightmare so immediate, she would sometimes check her stomach, just to assure herself of the smooth, unblemished skin.

That didn't help.

She started to jog to see if that would help ease some of the perpetual restlessness, the ultrasensitivity to noises and atmospheres in her. She started out lightly, increasing her speed and distance each day very slightly, and she felt her muscles toning up, tightening, sometimes painfully. She'd come back home, panting and blood pounding, but she couldn't seem to exorcise the devil that was riding her back.

All her senses were taut, vibrating. She saw things too clearly, she heard things too sensitively, and once when her mother brushed her arm accidentally, the reverberations of that human touch shivered through her. She was living too intensely, by the edge of that pit, constantly desperately concentrating on whatever came her way, because she knew that she would fall into the pit sooner or later. She was living like there was no tomorrow, like her death was to be that night, or that very next day, never stopping, never slowing, and the constant, rapid clicking of her brain as it stored information on every needless sound and incident and feeling was like the inexorable ticking of a timer on a bomb. She was living too high, too hard, as if she'd taken a drug and was flying though she knew the crash would come.

She wondered what a nervous breakdown felt like.

Monday morning, she took her new drawing pad

and roamed around outside, sketching small wildlife, and anything else that happened to catch her eye. She passed the morning in that fashion and then made her way back to the house at lunchtime, pleased with her morning's work. She was good and she knew it, but she wasn't so conceited as to think she held any particular genius. She knew better than that. She did know, however, that she could draw, and she spread out all of her drawings on the kitchen table to show her mother, who seemed impressed.

'I thought I might try something a little more ambitious,' Dana began, hesitantly, and was rewarded with a surprised and approving smile. Encouraged, she went on, 'I rather thought I might get together a collection of my wildlife drawings and do them in ink, perhaps splashing a little colour on a few. It would be hard work, I—I've never worked in ink before, but it sounds fun, doesn't it?'

'You know how I respect your work, Dana,' her mother replied, leaning against the kitchen counter and letting her eyes roam over the various sketches while she sipped from a coffee cup. 'And you know that you're good. You've never been anything but honest with yourself. What were you planning on doing with the ink drawings after you've finished with them?'

She shrugged. 'I really don't know. Maybe I could get them displayed in a bookstore or an art store somewhere. I was thinking about trying that. But first I have to get the drawings done!' She paused and then glanced at her mother, noticing with affection how Denise's hair was beginning to silver. It was striking against her dark hair. 'Do you really think they might sell?'

Her mother's response was immediate and sincere. 'Yes, I do. Your drawings have a sensitivity and a delicacy about them that is tremendously appealing. I think you have a great deal of promise.'

'Thanks.' Dana smiled slightly at the encouragement and praise from her mother, and Denise breathed an unconscious sigh of relief. It was the first real smile she'd seen from Dana in days.

But then the smile was fading and Dana's eyes went unfocused as her head came up like a questing dog's, sniffing the wind. She said briefly, 'The front door. Would you get it, Mom? I don't really feel like talking to anyone today.'

And Denise frowned, saying, 'Sure, I'll take care of whoever it is.' She noted the pallor in Dana's cheeks and the way her fingers tightened on her drawing pad. 'Is everything all right, dear?'

'Oh, yes,' she answered, too quickly. She tried to smile again, but it was the same facial movements that Denise had seen for the past three weeks. The older woman knew a sinking feeling. 'What could possibly be wrong?'

After staring at her daughter hard, Denise shook her head slightly and left to answer the knock at the front door that had not yet come. Dana kept her face averted until her mother had left the kitchen, and then she blew out a shaky sigh. She would steal out the back way while her mother talked to David Raymond. She knew that his intention was to speak to her and not her mother, but she had no desire to have what she was sure would be an unpleasant encounter with him. Then her head jerked, and her hand slipped on her pictures, sending them scattering to the floor.

'Oh, no,' she said in a kind of moan, panic fluttering through her stomach. 'He's coming for the back door, instead!' She'd felt him change his mind just as she'd known his original intent. It sent her scrabbling on the floor in a frantic effort to pick up all of her pictures and get out before he actually knocked. 'Mom! He's coming to the back door instead! Hurry and—oh, shoot!' That last was as a firm knock sounded not five feet away from where she was crouched. She straightened slowly, knowing she couldn't escape now since the curtains across the window in the back door were pulled wide open and that his eyes were on her.

She went to the back door and pulled it open reluctantly, just as her mother hurried into the kitchen from the front of the house. Dana lifted her eyes as if her gaze were under a heavy weight, and she met the dark, blank eyes of the silent man in front of her. He was still. Then he moved, breaking out of that silent pose. 'Hello, Dana,' David said quietly. 'May I come in, please?'

If Dana had been by herself, she would have been rude and refused, but her mother was standing there and watching, and Denise never tolerated rudeness to a visitor. Dana dropped her eyes and stepped back. She searched frantically for some kind of clue as to why he was there, feeling the air before her delicately, with invisible antennae, but she could pick up nothing aside from a grim purpose and the intention to speak to her. That unsettled her more than most anything else would have; she always relied on her extra sense like most people rely on their sight or their hearing. It was a mistake to do so, she knew suddenly. Sometimes it just didn't seem to work.

She had no inkling as to what to expect. She didn't know if he was angry or sad, or if he had anything on his mind other than a purely social call. No, that wasn't true. He wouldn't be so determined—and that she could sense—if he was merely paying a social visit.

Unknown to her, Dana's face had whitened considerably, and the skin under her eyes and around her fine nostrils was stretched tight from tension. David glanced at her assessingly and then looked across the room to her mother, who had stopped just inside of the kitchen doorway. 'My name's David Raymond,' he said smoothly, striding forward a few steps and holding out a browned, calloused hand. Denise shook it as he continued, 'I'm your new neighbour renting the house from Grace Cessler. I met your daughter a few days ago—last week sometime, wasn't it?' This was thrown over his shoulder to Dana's silent figure. She didn't bother to reply. 'We saw each other again at Grace's. I'm her cousin's grandson.'

'Oh, I see. Well, it's nice to meet you, Mr Raymond,' Denise replied, with every sign of enthusiasm. Dana could feel her sharpening interest in the man before her, and she felt almost hysterically amused at that. If her mother knew what she'd done already to this man! One thing was certain: he was not entertaining the kind of thoughts that Denise suspected. He most definitely didn't like her. She couldn't blame the man. For all he knew, she was a prying gossip. 'Would you like a cup of coffee, or perhaps some iced tea?'

Dana moved over quietly to the table and finished

stacking her drawings together, fully aware of the quick, questioning glance her mother had thrown to her. They were always careful as to whom they invited into their house because of Dana's sensitivity. Denise was asking her silently if everything was all right.

It was too late for that. The invitation had already been issued. Dana made a quick decision. She couldn't explain her behaviour to David, and so they really had nothing to discuss. She waited to hear what he would say to her mother, hoping uselessly that he would refuse.

But of course he didn't. He thanked her mother very courteously, accepting a glass of iced tea, and drinking the liquid with pleasure.

Dana said briefly, 'If you would please excuse me. I have many things to do.' She gathered her papers together, nodded pleasantly but distantly to David, avoided her mother's eyes and headed to the door.

She wasn't to get away so easily. David asked her quietly, 'May I have just a moment of your time? I won't take long, I promise. I have something I'd like to talk to you about.'

She turned and stared into his eyes, and she saw that they weren't quite as dark as they first appeared. The chocolate tone to his irises was highlighted by a lighter shade of honey towards the middle. She had to give him credit for tactfulness, she thought, nodding reluctantly. He'd managed to convey to Denise, very nicely, that he wanted a private talk. She was quick to take the hint, leaving after another quick, questioning glance to Dana.

When her mother's footsteps had died down, Dana

went jerkily to the coffee maker and went about the motions of starting the machine. She whisked down a cup, and when the brew was finished, she poured it quickly into her cup, all in a totally unnerving silence. Some spilled over on to the counter and she wiped it up, moving as jerkily as she'd poured. She couldn't stay still under that steady gaze.

'I talked to Grace quite a bit after you'd left on Thursday,' David said suddenly, and she jumped so violently at the sound of his voice that she spilled her coffee, again, and made a small choking sound as she burned her hand. Her lower lip trembled and she sucked a throbbing knuckle as she heard him move, setting down his glass sharply and coming over to her. Her cup was taken and set down also on the table—he didn't spill it—and the towel she'd used to mop up the mess was thrown on the floor to the spilled liquid there. Then he grabbed her hand and pushed it under the faucet, holding it there with his hand on her wrist. It was warm, encircling the thinness of her forearm completely, and a contrast to the cold wetness splashing on her hand.

She kept her face down, turned away from him as she started to shake. He had to feel it, she knew, because it wasn't a mere inward trembling that sometimes accompanies nervousness or self-consciousness. It was a violent shaking that came from severe emotional upheaval. His hand tightened briefly on her arm and then left it to come around her shoulders as he muttered, 'Oh, no. Don't shake so. Please don't shake.' Her hand had cooled under the water flow until it was almost numb, and she turned off the faucet and wiped her hands dry. Then he steered her to the table and pushed her into a chair, seating himself beside her. She took her coffee cup and stared into it, sipping from it and doing her level best to get steadier, but she didn't seem to do any good. She trembled like a leaf caught in a strong wind, and he saw it.

It was odd that she wasn't picking up those waves of dislike from him anymore. As she tried again to grope outwards for his mood, he asked her, 'What's wrong, Dana?'

'Nothing, I burnt my hand,' she replied expressionlessly. She wouldn't look at him. She was so vulnerable, too vulnerable. Anyone could come along and rip her apart inside, a kind of mental rape, and she couldn't do anything to stop it. She was wide open to any hurt David might inflict, all unknowingly. She was so full of her own emotional uncertainties that she didn't even notice how strange it was that he would start an intimate conversation with a near stranger.

'Something's wrong,' he said, still being gentle. 'But I won't push it. You're all right, though?' She nodded, and wondered why he would care to ask. Then she wondered if she had lied or not. He continued, 'I wanted to give you a bit of breathing space, so I put off coming over for a few days. I've wanted to come over and ask you a few questions, though. Grace told me quite a few things on Thursday.' He paused, seemingly to pick his words, and she felt the careful, hard control he exercised over his feelings. He was clamping down hard on them, keeping them firmly in rein. She caught the edge of something like a whiplash, though, and flinched away from him violently. The man had an incredible amount of strong emotion just waiting to burst from him like a geyser. He was the bomb she felt ticking away in her brain, and he was going to blow sky-high.

'What is wrong with you?' she whispered, and covered her mouth with trembling fingers, aghast at how she'd let herself slip in front of him, again. She pushed back her chair, abruptly, and it would have fallen except for his lightning swift grab. He righted it as she backed away, muttering, 'Excuse me, I'm not feeling well . . .' And she would have turned to run but for another of his lightning swift movements. Suddenly he was right in front of her and he had a hold on her arms.

'You're perfectly well,' he said in a quick, low voice. 'You're just upset. Why are you so upset, Dana?' The question had a hard urgency to it that she felt even in the midst of her turmoil, and she stared at him in surprise. 'What are you feeling right now? What kind of thoughts are going through your mind?'

Her eyes widened on him as she felt thunderstruck. *He knew!* ripped through her mind, followed by an agonised, *How?* 'Why do you want to know?' she asked, hopelessly dissimulating. 'Who am I to you? Why should you care what in the world I'm feeling?'

He sighed, the movements heaving his chest, and she had a brief instant of wonder at the new sensation of being so close to a powerful male body. It felt warm and different, not at all like she remembered feeling when she was held or hugged by her father. It felt . . . strange, but then everything about this man was strange. She put it down to that and then shrugged it away. It was just another strange emotion, coming from him. It was certainly nothing she'd ever felt before.

'Dana, I don't know how to say this,' he said deeply. 'But when Grace and I talked, what we discussed was how you'd known when she was hurt without having any way of knowing it. We talked about your sensitivity to other people and what they were feeling. We talked about how you'd known just when your father was killed, without anyone ever telling you.'

She wasn't sure what shocked her the most, the fact that Mrs Cessler had known for years the secret she'd tried so hard to keep, or that she had told this man, of all people. She broke away from him, crying out in agitation, 'I don't know what you're talking about! I didn't know anything of the sort!' Even as she spoke the lie, she knew it was hopeless. And her lie was so pathetic.

'You do know what I'm talking about,' he replied quietly, and the contrast between his quietness and her agitation was revealing in itself. She backed up and jolted into the wall behind her. 'And it does have to be talked about, so it won't do any good to prevaricate. Look, are you all right?' This was as she turned so completely white, she looked as though she might faint.

'I think you'd better go, Mr Raymond,' she said, and all her efforts to sound hard merely sounded quavering. She swallowed. 'I don't want to talk about this any longer. I don't know what you're talking about. I've never heard of anything like that before—I think you'd better go—' She sidled along the wall until she came to the doorway, backing through the open space and nearly screaming as she came up against someone there. She'd been so intent on watching the man in front of her, she hadn't even felt her mother's presence.

Denise's eyes were trained on David also, not her daughter. 'So you talked to Grace,' she said quietly. 'Why did you do that, Mr Raymond? What had Dana done?'

'Mother!' Dana hissed, and it was all too late anyway, but she was still hopelessly trying to make him disbelieve, to make him go away, like a grief stricken mother trying to make her dead child live by holding him tight. 'I—I think this conversation has gone far enough! Mr Raymond, will you please leave now?' Hardly aware of what she did, she backed away from her mother also, and she found herself in a corner, leaning against the counter and the wall.

'Dana, sweetheart, it's too late. He knows too much already—look, even I can see it in his eyes. And for some reason he needs to ask the questions. We can only hope that he's a good enough man to keep quiet about this, for our sakes.'

Dana wrung out both hands, twisting and turning them, clasping them so tightly together that the knuckles turned white and red from the pressure. Both of them were looking at her and they both looked so concerned and worried that she nearly couldn't stand it. Their feelings were hammering insistently at her now, for David was too emotionally aroused and involved to be able to hold on to his emotions well anymore, and Denise's worry rose to the fore like a weary spectre. The thoughts and the doubts and the worries and the fears were all too much for one person to take. She couldn't tell anymore what was her own and what was not. 'I—I'm not prepared for this,' she managed to stammer out, crossing her arms in front of herself in the age-old defensive gesture to cover nakedness. She glanced at her mother and felt the pity and the love from her so strongly that she nearly moaned aloud. Was she then such a freak, to be pitied thus? 'You haven't prepared me for this,' she whispered 'Sure, I was naked before, but nobody knew and now—now—' And at that incoherent, stammered statement, Dana did the only action left to her.

She turned and fled.

As she ran from the house, Denise sagged against the kitchen table with a gesture speaking of great tiredness, and her gaze travelled to the quiet man in front of her. There was no expression on his face, and she asked him, 'And what are you thinking now, Mr Raymond?'

Pale himself, he looked at the door that Dana had slipped out of, and he said softly, 'I'm thinking that I wish I hadn't had to force the situation.' He turned his head and looked at her, and though his face was devoid of feeling, she caught her breath at the depth of emotion in his eyes, feeling for a fleeting second a hint of what her daughter had felt her entire life. 'I'm thinking that I'd better follow her, to make sure she's all right.'

But Denise shook her head. 'No, I think you'd better give her a moment or two to calm down a bit, please. Give youself time to calm down, too. If you get near her in a state that is anything but calm, you'll do her more harm than good. She needs time to breathe— may I call you David? Good. I don't suppose you're going to tell me just why you are so involved in this, are you? She smiled, unsurprised as he shook his head wryly. 'I didn't think so. I'll just have to trust Grace's judgement, then. Oh, yes, I'd known that she had figured out something near to the truth when my husband died but until now everything has been better left unsaid. I hope you will be careful with Dana, whatever it is that you have to say to her. I hope that you are the kind of person to handle this kind of dangerous knowledge with wisdom and that you won't exploit her, like so many people would. She's been very sheltered.'

David just looked at the ground, his dark head bent, and something about his solid, broad shoulders and the look on his face made her relax even before he said, 'Mrs Haslow, I hope you can tell how sincere I am when I say that the last thing in the world I'd want to do is hurt your daughter, or anyone else.' His quick eyes flickered up to hers with a glimmer of smile in their dark chocolate depths, and as invulnerable as she knew herself to be to that sort of thing, Denise couldn't help an involuntary smile back at him. He was a very attractive man. 'And with your permission, I think I'd like to try to find your daughter now. I'm a bit worried about her.'

She found herself nodding. But as he started immediately for the door, she called after him, 'I don't believe you're going to have any success, though. There's a lot of wood out there, and Dana knows every inch of it. She won't be found unless she wants to be found.'

The back door swung shut and if he'd answered, it was lost in the slam of wood against hard wood.

The further that Dana travelled, the easier she was able to breathe. She still found herself trembling with dread and with something else. That tension inside of her was not just a wire pulled tight, but a shakingly delicate state of being. Anything touching that wire would, she thought, make it snap and then where would she be? Falling down into the pit? And what did the pit hold, craziness? Oblivion? An impenetrable depression?

She didn't want to know.

She climbed up a rising slope, having left any discernible path, and clambered up the rising ground until she reached the top of the hill and then she struck south, moving easily. The blue skies of summer hummed serenely above her with the sounds of living things. A jackdaw scolded, a squirrel chattered, and something rustled busily in the nearby bushes. She'd apparently walked too close, for a rabbit's composure broke, and he bounded from his cover in a silly, mindless panic, big eyes staring and ears twitching madly as great long feet thumped him away from the suspected danger. Stupid, cute little thing, she thought, watching him disappear. She smiled and continued on her way. If either her mother or David came after her, they wouldn't be able to find her. There was too much ground to cover and this was not one of her favourite haunts that she was known to frequent, which was precisely why she'd picked it. She cleared the trees, having come to a grassy clearing, and she sank to her knees. Only her head and shoulders were above the long, tangled green strands. The sun pulsed down, she could nearly hear its beating, it was so palpable. She let her muscles relax, feeling incredibly weary. Emotional states are so hard to sustain, and when she caught the lash of another's upheaval, it always would wring her dry inside.

She took a deep, easy breath, as if she was lacking oxygen. All of her life she'd lived in as much of a cocoon as her parents could weave around her. She felt so stifled suddenly she could barely breathe, and she yearned intensely to go out and experience life with gusto. And yet for her it was like a moth's attraction for deadly, beautiful flames. It could kill her if she succumbed to it. So she stood outside of the magic circle, not knowing the incantation that would get her in, watching achingly while life and her own youth slipped by like water trickling through fingers, wistfully wanting to be near people but unable to be near them. How balanced would she be if she happened to befriend someone with suicidal tendencies? What would happen if she got psychically involved with someone like that and became so empathetic that she would die also? Would she become totally unbalanced and commit suicide in the midst of another person's depression? It was the rhetorical question of her life, and one she dared not find the answers to.

She huddled into a small bundle. It was so close, like that black pit, so very close . . .

'May I join you?' David asked, his voice coming from behind her. Her head snapped up. Strange, to feel surprise. She rarely got surprises of that sort.

'How on earth did you know where to find me, for Heaven's sake?' she asked, unable to keep the astonishment out of her voice. Grass rustle. He dropped easily down beside her.

'So you occasionally miss with that radar of yours?' he asked in return, smiling at her. She mentally sniffed at the air, finding a soothing lack of turbulence. She relaxed.

'It's by no means infallible. I can't control it or direct it very well. Either it happens with a person or it doesn't and never will. Alack and alas, I can't even block it.' She drew in a deep breath then, amazed at herself.

'Please don't be distressed because I know,' he said carefully, and she knew he was trying to be gentle for her sake. 'I won't do anything to hurt you. I know it must be very frightening at times for you, and hard. If you'd rather just take a little time to adjust to me knowing about it, we can just be quiet, or I could leave. I don't want to upset you. I just came to see if you were all right.'

She smiled at him at that, incredibly touched, and saw him stare with an arrested look. But before she could wonder at what he was feeling, the look was wiped away as carefully and as cleanly as someone clearing a slate. She in turn stared. It seemed he was very good at control, then. 'You haven't told me how you found me,' she reminded him. 'Did I do something incredibly obvious, like track mud or white paint?'

A flash of amusement at that, barely shown but swiftly caught by her, like a tossed ball. 'No. I don't know. I just started to randomly search around. Intuition, I suppose.' At her stare, he had to chuckle, a rumbling sound in his chest. 'An odd word to someone like you, I'll bet. No, nothing came down out of the sky like a lightning bolt. I simply wandered around, and hit on you by luck.'

'I—see. Oh, I see what you mean. Yes, it's a bit hard for me to believe in a vague thing like luck when it's more definite for me. I guess I'm continually surprised when other people don't sense the things that I do.' Her eyes fell away and she reached out to pluck absently at the grass. The harshness of the green strands slit into her skin slightly. 'It's lonely.'

His hand came out quickly at that and took hold of hers, and after the first startled jump, she let her stiff fingers relax in his warm grip. 'Would it help to talk about it?' he asked quietly. 'All of that input into that small body and hardly anyone to listen to the output . . .'

Her vision blurred and the leaf she'd been concentrating on vanished into water. 'I don't know.' It was a quickly whispered, almost ashamed admission. His fingers tightened.

'Grace told me that you must have felt it when she fell down the stairs. Did you feel her pain, or did you hear her cry out with your mind? How did you know?' he asked her, and she glanced at him with something like apprehension.

'You—you don't disbelieve any of this, do you? I mean, you really think this is real. You aren't laughing at me?' She couldn't for some strange and perverse reason sense anything from him right at the moment, and she felt the frustration of knowing that when she wanted to she couldn't seem to force her extra sense to work, while at other times she couldn't get it to stop.

'I'd like to,' he replied, after a hesitation. 'It would be more comfortable for me if I could. But I have too much respect for that picture you drew and for Grace's observations, and your own mother's utter and familiar certainty. And mostly I respect those painfully honest eyes you're turning on me right at the moment. I most seriously believe you.'

She sighed and felt the weight of a life-long fear slip off her slim shoulders. 'I've always been afraid that if someone were to find out about me, they would scoff. You see, it's something so utterly and immediately— there to me. It's my reality.'

He picked up her train of thought easily, and it was as if they were old friends instead of two people just getting to know one another. 'And no one likes to have their version of reality ridiculed. Trusting someone's opinion is a dying trait in this world, I'm afraid.' His fingers played with hers idly, and she flushed at the intimate contact, furious at herself for flushing and still unable to help it. She suddenly remembered her agitation when he'd been so close a short time ago, and suddenly the age-old premise that she'd been leaning on was not so sure anymore as she realised that the unfamiliar emotion was coming from herself and not him.

'I'm sorry I blurted out what I did on Thursday,' she offered hesitantly. 'If it had been anyone but Grace, I would have just died—'

He interrupted her. 'Forget it. It's understandable, now that I know a little better about what goes on in that little head of yours.'

'Forgivable, too, I hope.'

'As long as you forgive my unpleasantness,' he returned, and she heard the smile in his voice.

She smiled involuntarily, echoing his words to her, 'It's understandable. Forget it. There's nothing to forgive.' A bird winged by overhead and she lifted her head to stare up after it. The sun was full in her eyes as she looked straight up and for a split instant all she was aware of was golden white blindness, the downward beat of the summer warmth, a hand whose strength she could guess at by the very carefulness by which it was cradling hers, and the fresh smell of green, growing grass. Then she looked down and the world shifted back into visual awareness.

David was asking her, 'That night we first met, did you sense me in the trees or did I somehow make a noise you heard? I could have sworn that I was being quiet and was very surprised when you knew I was there. I'd wanted to watch you to find out if you'd had dishonourable intentions towards the house, and I was planning a few nasty surprises of my own.'

Dana looked at the grass right in front of her, where a beetle was assiduously and earnestly climbing up a long thin blade of grass. The grass bent, and the beetle fell to the ground. It picked itself up and started to blindly climb again, this time on a different blade of grass. She wondered where it was going to, or if it even knew. 'I didn't hear you,' she said quietly.

'And you weren't afraid?' His tone was strange. She looked at him quickly and found him, not watching her as she'd suspected, but looking off into the wood as if he would see some answer to a vitally important question. He looked tired, and she realised that many of the lines on his face were from exhaustion, not age. He couldn't be much older than thirty-five or so. It didn't seem old to her. And she wondered with a bit of a jolt if she'd ever been young.

'No,' she said, and this time the quietness in her voice was firm. 'There was nothing in that night that would have hurt me.' She felt him relax and tried to guess at what she'd said to reassure him. Her eyes travelled to her hand, clasped in his. 'Do you know,' she said, almost at random, 'how fascinating mythology can be?' His attention caught, he turned his head to look at her, trying to figure out the change of subject. 'I've just reread the myth of Eurydice and Orpheus. Do you know it? I've always been struck at how he travelled all the way to Hades just to bring her back to life, because he loved her so.' Her eyes filmed over with dreaminess and she whispered musingly. 'It seems everybody gets to some version of hell, some time in their life. I guess it's just that some of them make it back.'

It was as if she'd struck him, he was so still. And suddenly she was overwhelmed with the desire to get away from him, from everyone, and just be alone. She was so unused to having someone look at her exposure. She tugged her hand away and stood abruptly. 'I'm sorry,' she said to him, voice slightly unsteady. His head had jerked up. She backed away. 'Excuse me. I don't mean anything personal about this, it's just—just—I need to be by myself . . .' She looked at him pleadingly, and something in his eyes softened. 'I know you wanted to talk, but c—could we leave it right now?'

He just smiled a queer, twisted smile and said quietly, 'You need time. You weren't expecting anything like this, were you?' He hesitated. 'Who am I to say one way or another, after all? You don't mind me knowing, do you?'

'I guess I do,' she said uncertainly. 'But it's not anything we have any control over anymore, is it? I— what was it you wanted to talk about, anyway?'

She watched him as his face shuttered up and blanked every expression out, something coming over his thoughts like a dark blanket. She thought of those terrifying nightmares and the horrible dread when she woke from them, and she thought she understood. It wasn't easy to talk about, those dreams. She'd never even told her mother what they were about. 'You see?' she said, shrugging with a gesture that was unconsciously helpless. 'You need time as much as I. Only,' and her eyes raised to the sun as something dark shadowed her vision, 'only I can't help but wonder how much time we have left.'

She wasn't even aware of how she had used the plural instead of singular in that last muttered statement, and though his head came up sharply and his eyes widened, he didn't tell her.

CHAPTER FOUR

DANA dragged her feet through the grass as she walked back to her house alone. She tried in vain to recapture some sense of peace or tranquillity, some sense of what she'd been like last month, or a few weeks ago. She couldn't. Something was changing in her, and it only partially had something to do with the nightmares that she was so mentally receptive to.

It had quite a lot to do with David Raymond. He seemed to be the cause, or the catalyst for many of the unfamiliar feelings inside of her, and the differences. She'd reached a new plateau of living; she'd taken a step in growth, and it was a measure of her seclusion and isolation that she was somewhat surprised to find herself and her awareness shifting. She had taken a step forward and now, looking back, she saw another girl in the past, the girl that she had been. She could no longer identify with that girl. It seemed to be the difference between an adolescent and an adult.

Forced as she was to empathise with another, strange adult, she'd managed to mature in some way. She was no longer in a glass cage looking out, no longer the lone princess in the castle. She hadn't realised how little she'd empathised with her mother, close though they were. Perhaps it was that very closeness that had caused them to keep somewhat distant. Whatever the reason, Dana found that she really was a world apart from her mother, and that was

71

a new and strange feeling, one that she'd never thought to have. Adolescent rifts with the parent had always happened to someone else, but never to Dana. She'd known too much, had been too aware of what was going on, at least that was what she'd thought. Now, looking back, she had to smile wryly as she recognised in herself for the first time that typical adolescent arrogance. She'd known it all, then. She was an old woman in a teenager's body, and nobody knew it. She was the authority, the ultimate in worldly cynicism and weary wisdom. She was so young.

Dana was beginning to see just how normal she was in some aspects, and it was laughable in a way. She stopped walking and propped herself up on a waist high rock, staring at the pattern of fallen pine needles, brown and dry, that cushioned the forest floor. How deflating it was to recognise something like that! She was the special one, the freak, the different and unique one. That had always been her pride and despair, the source of both her joy and sorrow.

And now she was finding that she wasn't so different after all. She was finding that she didn't recognise the feelings that David Raymond prompted in her, either from the store of her own experiences or the wealth of her vicarious knowledge. It was just something she knew nothing about. It was an attraction she'd never before dreamed could exist.

And there, it was out in her consciousness now. She looked at the thought, mentally sniffed at it and examined it from all sides and reluctantly had to admit it was true. She was attracted to David. It was an attraction different from anything she'd known. It wasn't just the attraction for a kindred spirit or a likeable person, it was much more than that; there was something elemental about it, something having to do with the fact that he was a personable male and she liked that maleness of him, that alien quality that complemented her femininity. She liked the man on different levels. She liked his mind and that he was a strong man of deep emotions and hard control. She liked his fairness and his ability to understand something outside of his experience, and sympathise. She liked how he was able to really listen to what was said and not just hear the words. She liked how he had reached out to cradle her hand when he thought she needed support, how he was secure in himself enough to offer the support right then instead of merely feeling uncomfortable and looking away, like so many people did. And last of all, that unfamiliar feeling she was only now experiencing, wholly on her own and for the first time in her life, that quite frankly attraction to his masculinity.

Self-conscious at the newness of it and the unexpected awareness of her own femininity, she shrugged a little and laughed under her breath, hopping down from the rock. It was silly. He very probably didn't notice her at all. The one thing she could do without right at the moment was a typical case of adolescent infatuation, on top of everything else. That was what she feared it was, for her confidence in herself was badly shaken at her new and deeper self-knowledge.

She devoutly hoped that she wouldn't make a fool of herself.

Back at the house, Dana found her mother busy in the kitchen, making supper. She closed the door quietly on the evening swarm of bugs, watching as her mother quickly turned and came forward immediately. She could feel the older woman's concern and smiled reassuringly. 'I just needed some breathing space, Mom. What are we having for supper?'

Denise searched her daughter's pale, tired face. 'You're sure you are all right? Did David manage to find you after all?'

'Yes, he did,' Dana replied, a slight frown creasing her brow. 'Which was surprising to me, but then random occurences do happen.' A lightning quick, half smiling glance at her mother. 'I was trying to remain private, you see, and hadn't realised that I could be found as easily as that.' She went over to the refrigerator and took out the milk, pouring herself a full glass and draining it thirstily.

Denise went back to the stove and Dana peered over her shoulder at the spaghetti sauce she was making. Dana could sense that there were still questions that her mother wanted to ask her, but all she said was, 'Is everything all right, Dana? You're okay?'

She took a great big breath and then heaved it in a sigh, feeling the ever present weight of that dangerous tension and the fine tremor in her hands. 'I don't know.' She didn't look up as her mother glanced at her sharply. 'I wish I could say yes, but there's something happening that I don't understand and can't control.' She shrugged again and said helplessly, 'I don't know.'

Denise stirred the sauce and put down the large spoon very carefully, as if the precise position of the spoon on the stove top was hugely important. 'It's something to do with David, isn't it?'

Dana jerked and she was glad that her mother wasn't looking at her to see the tell-tale reaction. She'd nearly spilled her milk. She could have told the truth. She could have said yes. But all she said was, again, a rather miserable, 'I don't know.'

Denise said softly, 'I'm worried about you.' And Dana privately agreed. She was worried about herself, too. She made a move to sit down at the table and then stopped and turned around to look at her mother.

'Do you know who I'm worried about?' she asked. 'I think I'm worried about David.' She wondered why her mother felt and looked so surprised.

'Are you really? I wouldn't be,' Denise said, smiling slightly. 'That's a man who won't lose control, if I'm any judge of character. He has a good hold on himself.'

That's what I'm worried about, she thought, and wondered why the thought had come out of the blue like it had. It was true, but she hadn't really seen it as a danger before. She rather saw it as something to be envied, a trait she wished she had, that ability to lock oneself away, to click in a remote part of oneself away from all of the outside influences and inputs, to be able to divorce oneself from one's most dangerous and overwhelming emotions. It seemed a characteristic that could be potentially harmful, if one became locked away too tightly and got trapped. All of those repressed emotions would seethe and boil away under the surface until something blew apart. There had to be an outlet as well as a refuge in oneself. She wished she had that kind of control, though. She didn't have a problem with her own emotional output so much as

she did her input. She was all on the surface, too close
to the open air, her vulnerable self exposed.

That night Dana had another dream. It was not a
screamingly horrifying nightmare. It was just quietly
frightening. She dreamed that there was something after
her in the dark, something silently stalking. She could
never rest or sit down, though she was so very tired. She
knew that if she could keep awake and ahead of that
something, she would be all right. She had good reflexes
and was quick on her feet. But the problem was that she
was so very tired. She knew that if she went to sleep, she
would die. And she knew at the same time that she was
dreaming, but she couldn't make herself wake up. All
she could do was sweat it out, that eternity of stalking
and being stalked, trying to get back home to the safe
place. But there was no safe place. Nothing was safe.
Everything was, however, very dark.

In time the dream faded away and she was able to
sleep on undisturbed the rest of the night. But when
she woke up she remembered that dream, though she
didn't understand it.

Dana ripped out of bed and got dressed as quickly
as she could, not understanding why she felt such an
urgent need to get covered. She grabbed her clothes
out of the closet, a tan pair of slacks and an olive green
shirt, and put on her comfortable tennis shoes. After
she had finished, she felt a bit better and she went
down to the kitchen to fix herself some kind of
breakfast. Instead of cooking herself something, she
went to the cupboard and found a can of peaches and
had them with milk. She ate quickly, wolfing down
her food though she had no appetite. She'd need the
energy later. She had to get done quickly.

Her head hurt and that was strange, for she rarely got headaches of any kind, but her head was definitely hurting now and she rubbed her temples irritably. Her mother walked into the kitchen right at that moment and saw her.

'Good morning, dear. What's wrong? Do you have a headache?' Denise asked her, patting her briefly on the shoulder as she went by.

Dana sighed shortly. 'Yes. I think it's from the heat. At least it feels like it's from the heat. I don't know.' She barely noticed her mother's raised eyebrows.

'That's funny,' Denise said slowly, watching Dana. 'I'm not hot at all. We're supposed to have a fairly mild day today, from the weather reports.' She came up to Dana and put her fingers on her daughter's forehead. 'You don't seem to have a fever.'

Dana shook off her mother's hand. 'No, no, I'm fine. I just have a headache and I'm a little warm, that's all. I'll take some aspirin and be fine. Do we have any salt tablets?'

'Salt tablets—for what?' her mother asked, astonished.

She blinked. 'Nothing. For nothing.' She shook her head and winced at the throbs of pain. 'I'm not sure where that came from.' She smiled at her mother, trying to hide how her heart was pounding and her palms were sweating. It was like an anxiety attack, or a surge of adrenalin, and she licked dry lips. Suddenly she needed action and she stood up. 'I think I'm going to walk to the store this morning, instead of waiting until tomorrow. I need the exercise. Is there anything special you'd like me to buy?'

Her mother was still watching her, slightly

frowning, unsure. Dana didn't look at her and she said slowly, 'There's nothing that really can't wait. I'd rather you didn't go just yet, dear. Dana, what—what's going on?'

She heard her mother ask the question and she heard herself reply, as if she were someone else. 'I'm splitting wide open.' Her hand crept up to her throat, as if surprised at what she'd said, as if to hold back the words. She shook her head again to try to clear out the cobwebs, her vision clouding. 'I don't know, Mom. There's something racing along inside of me that I can't stop, like a snowball falling down a hill, going to someplace and building up momentum, I——' Her eyes sharpened on her mother's worried visage. '—I need some action. I'll be back in a little bit.'

And with that, in spite of her mother's protests, Dana got some money out of her purse and left the house, heading for the store. Maybe she would stop at the post office and get some stamps. They only had a few left and they would be paying bills soon. Her eyes travelled to the sky and she felt a drop of sweat trickle down the side of her face. Maybe she would stop at the drug store and pick up some salt tablets. She wouldn't be surprised if it broke a hundred degrees today.

Back in the house, Denise stood and bit at her lip in indecision. Then she made up her mind and picked up the phone book by the telephone, her finger travelling down a list of names until she reached Mrs Cessler's phone number. She then picked up the receiver and dialled quickly, hoping that David hadn't seen fit to change the number when he moved in. She stood there for a very long time, listening to the phone ring on and on, with no one there to answer.

Dana wandered on down the pavement, not really paying attention to anything around her. She was lost in her own thoughts, struck by a mental image. She felt that tight wire inside of her, but now she rather fancied herself walking over the taut, vibrating wire, and the wire was stretched over the pit. She shrugged off such fanciful thinking as she realised that she was in front of the store. The post office was across the street. She headed there first since she could put the stamps in her pocket and she didn't fancy juggling her packages while trying to buy stamps. As she paid for them rather absentmindedly, her head snapped up like a leash being pulled tight on her neck.

Something was happening outside. Someone was distressed—she didn't know who. It was someone young. She hurried outside, looking up and down the street, shading her eyes from the summer sun. There was no one there. Dana checked the street and then jogged across, not really sure where she was going, hunting the air for a location.

Something was close, something dangerous, something wild. Her steps slowed and then she went on, walking now. Not something, but someone.

She quietly turned the corner, making for the blind alley behind the grocery store, sure now where she was going, and sure of who she would find. Someone whimpered, a girl's frightened cry, and Dana came upon the two people, Mick and a girl she didn't know but who looked very young. Perhaps fifteen, no more. The girl was backed against the wall and Mick stood over her, menacing and overpowering, but in the instant they both became aware that Dana was there, he immediately became nothing more than a young man, out to tease a young girl.

But Dana knew better, because she didn't rely on appearance but rather undercurrents, and what she most definitely sniffed from that young girl was the stench of fear. She smiled a slow cold smile and walked casually forward. 'Hello, Mick. Nice day, isn't it? What are you up to today, hmn?' And as she spoke, she deliberately walked right up to him, stared him in the eye, forcing him to fall back an automatic step. She was then right by the girl, and she put out a hand without looking, feeling a cold and trembling hand creep into hers. She squeezed.

Mick then smiled unpleasantly. He was taller than Dana by half a head and looked strong. 'Why, if it isn't the little Miss Snob! What're you doing back here, anyway—come to check out the garbage?'

Dana looked him up and down, feeling a cold wave of anger so intense, it shook through her like a storm. 'It appears to me,' she said slowly, 'that the garbage is just fine. Stinks, as usual.' She turned her head to the young girl and smiled down at her. 'But what I'd like to know is why such a young thing like you is back here with all the garbage?'

The other girl stammered out something, but Dana didn't catch what it was for Mick interrupted nastily, 'Don't believe a word of what she says. She wanted to come back here! No matter what you may think, I didn't force her back here!'

Dana looked at him, her eyes very brilliant and still very cold, like clear washed emeralds. She sensed too many things, and she had to stand still to decipher them, trusting her own senses over anything Mick told her. She sensed his fury at her appearance, mingled with that flicker of danger and sheer, utter boredom, coming from a reckless young man with little or nothing to do. She sensed the fear coming from the young girl and it was that of a trapped animal, mingled with a sense of shame. Mick was telling the truth, as far as it went. She looked at the other girl thoughtfully. 'Well, I certainly hope that you've learned your lesson,' she said mildly, letting go of the small hand she'd had clasped. 'And it looks like you've been frightened enough, so why don't you just get out of here and go home, hm? Or at the very least, stay out of trouble and stick with someone your own age.'

The girl scuttled away like a frightened rabbit, and Dana turned back to lash Mick one more time with her contemptuous eyes before preparing to leave, herself. But even as she turned away, she knew she wasn't going to make it, so she wasn't surprised when Mick's heavy hand came down and clamped on her arm, throwing her around to face him. That dangerous quality she had sensed in him had come to the fore. As she hit the wall facing him, though she hadn't been surprised, her heart started to pound and her mouth dried out with a kind of fear she'd never felt before. He was bigger than she, and his shove had contained a lot of physical power in it. But she faced him with every appearance of nonchalance, though the danger was like a bad taste in her mouth.

'You've butted in where you're not wanted, sister,' he said softly, eyes glittering strangely as he looked her up and down, appraisingly. The look was coldly sexual, and degrading. 'Are you willing to take the consequences, I wonder?'

'Back off!' she snarled, the fury in herself growing and spilling out at his encroachment. How dared he? And in that split second, realisation flashed into her mind with the force of a lightning bolt. It wasn't just Mick who was emanating that danger. It was herself. She was dangerous. She barely blinked an eye outwardly, though she was seething inside, and she continued in a soft voice that made Mick's eyes widen. 'You aren't intimidating a young girl anymore, and I suggest you re-evaluate what you're getting yourself into. You're deeper than you think. Now, let me pass.'

The widened look in the young man's eyes dissipated, along with his look of perpetual boredom, into something like excitement. Dana felt his interest quicken, and she began to feel quite alarmed, backing up as far as she could to get away from him. This was not merely the obnoxious young man who would plague her occasionally for the sheer devilment of it. This was an animal; something, she sensed fearfully, ready to throw off the bounds that society pressed on it. 'Why, I might let you by,' he drawled slowly, coming forward until she was backed against the wall much in the same way that the other girl had been. 'If you can give me the right kind of password, or—well,' and he smiled, 'the equivalent thereof. Come on, sweetheart. So you're not the young thing that I was teasing a moment ago. That's all the better. You're old enough to play in the big league now, aren't you?' And he reached out an idle-seeming hand to wrap a strand of her thick hair around his finger.

He was much too close. She swept out a stiffened arm and knocked his hand away from her so violently that he bit off a muttered exclamation, and her head

jerked as he took some of her hair with him. She bit
out between her teeth, 'You keep your hands to
yourself, little boy. I don't like it—they're all muddy.
Now, get out of my way before I take half of your face
off with my fingernails.'

She pushed past him, knowledge sick within her:
she knew he wouldn't stand for this; she knew he was
going to react aggressively, even as she made the move
to get away. It was a hopeless attempt to get out of the
situation, and everything inside of her was taut,
vibrating, don't touch the wire, Mick, don't touch it or
it'll snap, don't touch me . . .

. . . And his hand came down on to her shoulder
again, heavily, fingers biting cruelly into her slender
collarbone, the pressure swinging her violently
around, his face contorted into a mask of rage which,
compared to what was about to blow up inside of her,
was just a mere childish tantrum. As she came around,
her arm shot up and her hand cracked across his cheek
as hard as she could hit. The fingers in her hand
numbed as his head snapped back, and then he
slammed her against the wall.

She hit the concrete with her shoulder, bruising
herself to the bone and crying out. There was no time
to think right then, all she could do was turn her head
and look at Mick as he came for her, both hands
shooting out and aiming for her neck as he intended to
grab her and yank her to him.

Something snapped in her head; the wire broke;
everything in the world seemed to click over into
something else, something different. The entire reality
of the world as she knew it shifted. Her eyes widened
in horror as she watched Mick's hands coming at her

in slow motion. Then, strangely, she was seeing two people where Mick was standing, one of them odd looking, foreign. He had come at her in that very same way, seemingly to waver in the incredible, muggy heat, and she dropped down instinctively, her body jerking in an unfamiliar movement that was somehow hauntingly familiar too, and her stiff hand shot out to chop at his vulnerable neck. His head jerked, and she took the opportunity to go to her hands and knees, her leg sweeping out to knock him flat on his back. He lay there for a second, stunned, and she came to her feet as he rolled over. She whirled and started to run, and smacked right into a hard body that was coming their way. It was David, and he grabbed her shoulders to steady her, but she knocked them away and ran on, swiftly.

Mick in the meantime had rolled to his feet and had started to chase her, jerking up short as he saw that someone else was there in the alley. He stopped warily, chest heaving and eyes looking half wild as he stared at David askance.

David, with more than half of his mind on Dana and where she might be running to, moved quicker than a striking panther, his body a blur, and Mick was then pinned against the wall, choking, as David's forearm pressed mercilessly against the younger man's larynx. His teeth were showing in an unconscious snarl, and he looked incredibly dangerous. Mick started to stammer out something, all of his bravado washing down an invisible drain as he was no longer confronting a young girl or a smaller, weaker woman but a fully mature and powerfully built, angry man. David cut him short as he bunched his fists into the collar of Mick's shirt and shook him until his teeth rattled, then throwing him aside like a tossed mongrel pup, biting out harshly, 'I don't have time for this now. If I see you again, I'll ram my fist down your throat, do you hear me, boy?'

Mick's eager nod and quick reply was lost to David as he ran back through the alley, looking up and down the street alertly, dark eyes oddly vivid and his face, under its overlying habit of inscrutability, showing a hint of worry. Then his head went up, the action oddly like Dana's habitual sensing the air, the action wholly unconscious. He turned and loped up the street.

Dana was running as fast as she could, caught in the middle of a singularly odd crisis, propelled into it by that hauntingly familiar aggressive movement from Mick. Her chest heaved in huge, air sucking gasps, her face and bare neck and arms glistening with sweat. Her head jerked first to the left and then the right, searching for signs of danger.

Her whole perception had clicked over into something so very real to her, so utterly immediate and frighteningly present that she was in a state of panic. The landscape was different, her home, her whole world far, far away as she fought to survive in a place totally alien, bizarre, and threatening.

She had to get to those soldiers, had to find them as soon as possible. Five men, no, five mere boys, injured and alone in the rain forest would never survive all of the snipers, the guerrilla fighting, the damnable booby traps. If night fell and they were still out there, they might as well be dead. For that matter, so might she/ he. That 'copter crash had really shaken her/his world up. God knows, she/he didn't ever want to see another helicopter again in his life. After this, by God, he'd never fly again, not if he'd anything to say about it.

No weapons, no ammunition, no food, no medical supplies, no shelter—chances were, all of them would die tonight. If the Viet Cong didn't get him, then a Bouncing Betty would and just blow him to hell. God, this was senseless, a huge jungle full of creeping, sweating, panicked kids fighting dully on. There was absolutely no relief from it, the constant presence and danger of this stinking hole. There was nothing in this world but survival. And it wasn't any easier just because he was a few years older than most of the eighteen-year-old boys who were given guns and shown how to kill, and then shoved into a nightmare.

It didn't matter how old you were; you were never ready for anything over here. Violently killed people are dead, no matter how one looks at it. The blood was red, no matter who it came from.

Dana ran on, her mind working on two levels. On the very superficial level, she was seeing the strip of asphalt she was racing down and acknowledging its existence. But that level was fast disappearing as the other level of consciousness pushed to supremacy. It wasn't really there in the context of reality that she was now seeing. It was beneath her feet and yet different as she wandered in that disconnected reality that dreams and nightmares occupy. She passed a tree that she'd known for fifteen years, a good, solid oak, but it wasn't familiar anymore. Everything was enemy territory, alien landscape, different, sinister.

She'd overbalanced, and fallen in. This was the pit. This was where the nightmares had been heading, gradually sucking her in until she was no longer the observer but the participant, not merely sharing the dream but living it, with her fear and sweat and rage. She couldn't separate her own ego from the picture.

God, what a time for this to be happening to him! He was an old timer now, almost ready to be shipped back to the States. He had only a month and a half more to put in until he had served his time, and then he was going home. It was typical. All of the old timers got it just before they were to leave this hell-hole. Either that or they got it just after they came back from R&R.

If he ever got out of this place alive, he would never think, hear or talk of it again. He'd bury this so deep that no one would ever find it again, least of all him. He never wanted to remember this time. He'd never even breathe the name Vietnam.

It was all so senseless. It was all so futile and senseless.

CHAPTER FIVE

DANA burst into the house like a bullet, hurtling through the living room and racing madly for the stairs. She threw open the hall closet door and started to haul things out swiftly, cursing at her shaking hands as she fumbled. First she drew out a blanket and threw it on the floor, spread out. Then she started to throw things on it: the first aid kit, rolls of bandages, scissors, a few clean, white towels. Her mother, attracted by the noise, came out into the hall and stared at Dana, amazed.

'What on earth are you doing?' Denise demanded.

Sweat glistened on Dana's forehead. She barely heard her mother's question. It was a good thing this encampment was so close. She had to hurry before someone came upon her. Damn it, she had no weapon! What should she do—something sparked in her mind and she grabbed the edges of the blanket together and hauled it downstairs. Denise followed, beginning to feel alarmed.

'Dana, will you tell me what you think you are doing?' she repeated, grabbing a hold of her daughter's arm.

Dana threw it off violently. 'I crashed!' she shouted impatiently. 'I crashed before I could get to them! They're going to die if we don't get them to a MASH unit soon! Get the hell out of my way!' She had to try to make it to the unit with these supplies. It wasn't

much, but it could make the difference between life
and death for some of them. She ran into the kitchen
and swept like a fury through the cupboard, grabbing
cans of food at random and throwing them down with
the medical supplies. Then she pelted for the study,
yanking open drawers as she searched, leaving a wreck
behind her as they fell out to the floor when she pulled
too hard.

'Oh, my God!' Denise, ashen-faced, breathed. She
jumped forward, throwing out both hands. 'No, Dana!
Don't—don't do that . . . Oh, dear God . . .' Intent as
she was, horror-stricken at what Dana had found,
Denise didn't hear David crash into the house until he
was right behind her, pushing roughly past and
heading like an arrow for Dana only to be brought up
short as she slowly turned around and stared at him
with dilated eyes, her skin stretched light.

She was holding a black and deadly revolver in one
small hand, and she pushed the wheel back home.

She stared at David, a look of wild desperation in
her eyes, and her hands trembled on the small, heavy
gun. He was standing absolutely still, absolutely
white, his eyes leaping with emotion. He just looked at
her and there was something sick in his eyes. 'Dana,'
he said gently and quietly, making no move. 'Dana,
sweetheart, please listen to me. It's all right. You can
relax and put the gun down now. Please, can you
manage to give me the gun?' He advanced one step.

She just stared at him, eyes wide. *It was hot, so hot.
'Nam was just pure murder in the summertime, getting
unbearably humid and scorching. It was pure murder in
the winter, too, with the rainy season and the monsoons,
and water and mosquitoes everywhere. In fact, 'Nam*

was just plain murder, no matter how you looked at it. Kids murdering kids, and nobody was stopping it. Crazy, the whole world's gone crazy. She took a deep, shaking breath and mopped her forehead. Her hand came away wet. 'I forgot the salt tablets,' she whimpered, looking at the wetness on her hand.

David, eyes intent, heart leaping, took another step. She was across the desk, so far away. God, she looked so small and fragile and innocent, and she had that gun held so precariously in her hands. 'I've got some salt tablets, sweetheart,' he murmured, and he held out his hand. 'I have some at home. I'll give them to you, only you have to put the gun down to go with me. Please, Dana, put it down.' Oh, please.

Denise, terrified and frozen, could only watch David as he took another step. Dana's eyes suddenly sharpened on him fiercely, and she backed so sharply up against the bookcase that she cracked her sore shoulder against a protruding shelf and cried out in pain. Denise made a sound and covered her mouth with both shaking hands. David had frozen again.

The nozzle of the gun turned slowly to point right at David. Dana just shivered and shook, backed up against the wall in a classic example of sheer animalistic fear, her face near to crumpling into tears, lips trembling and eyes full of sickness.

'Mrs Haslow,' David said quietly, never moving, 'is it possible that the gun is loaded, or do you know for a certainty that it's safe?'

'I don't know,' she whispered. 'It could be loaded. There were bullets in the cabinet and she had her back to me and was doing something to the gun. But I don't see how she would know to load it—she's never handled a gun in her life—she wouldn't know how to use it if she wanted to. What's wrong with her? She looks half dead from fright!'

'I think I'm afraid to find out,' he said reluctantly. He tentatively put out another foot and eased forward. Dana's eyes, like a cat's, never left him, unblinkingly. He asked her gently, 'Dana, what's happened? Why do you need the gun?'

'I—I crashed,' she whispered dully. 'I crashed the helicopter. They shot me down. I can't get to those poor kids, they—they're dying. I know they are.'

David looked and felt like he'd been hit unexpectedly in the stomach. He moaned something under his breath, queerly. Then he took a deep breath, the passage in his throat sounded ragged in the tense filled room. 'Oh, Dana, Dana—the kids are all right. I know, I've just come from there. I've seen them. You don't have to worry. The fighting's all over with. *Please* put down the gun. You're scaring your mother, see?'

'You're lying!' Dana screamed, and Denise screamed too. Only David was as still as a statue. Furiously, Dana continued, 'You're lying to me, damn you! I know they aren't all right! I was the only pilot free to answer their radio signals! *They're dying!* Those kids . . .' Her eyes, after misting over with such anguish that both Denise and David caught their breath at it, sharpened into such a look of fury and hate that her whole face was altered. She spat out, 'Get the hell out of my way! Move back from the door! Both of you, go on! Get over to that side of the room!'

Slowly both David and Denise complied. Dana's mother's face was so grey and full of fear that something in Dana's face flickered for a moment as a sliver of reality wedged into her nightmare. But it was gone again in a split second, and her face was full of desperation and futile determination.

Dana edged from behind the desk, opposite to the two watching her, and she slowly inched out of the door, never taking her eyes from them. Then she whirled and ran as fast as she could, forsaking her little bundle of supplies and breaking out of the door fast, hitting one of the many paths that converged to their lawn at a dead run. She had to find those kids and help them, she had to.

Back at the house, David took a deep, steady breath and then turned his attention to Denise, who looked suddenly older and completely colourless. He was alarmed at what he saw, and he took her gently by the arm and forced her to sit down. She stared up at him fearfully. 'What happened to her?' she asked. 'She's never been this way before, never! Oh, God, what if she hurts someone? David, we've got to stop her!'

'No—no, Mrs Haslow,' he said, making her sit still in the chair with both hands. 'Just take a few minutes and try to calm down a bit. Will you do that? Will you try to keep as calm as you can about this? I'll go and look for her. I promise, I'll find her, and everything will be all right.'

Denise stared at him and she saw the emotion that darkened his eyes, the expression of something horrifying that clung to him like a black clawed thing, how he was so utterly white. He was labouring under some terrific stress. 'What was Dana talking about when she said she crashed?' she asked him slowly, staring. He swallowed and her eyes sharpened. 'You know, don't you? This has something to do with you, doesn't it?' He didn't answer, and she said, seemingly to change the subject, 'I tried to call you when she left the house earlier. She was acting so strangely then, too, and I—I thought that maybe you could see her safely to the store and back, to make sure she was all right. But you weren't home.'

A muscle jerked in his jaw. His hands tightened on hers, tightened spasmodically and then, as he became aware of her stare, and his tight grip on her, he let go and stood back. 'I was coming over here,' he said flatly. Her eyes widened.

'Why? You surely didn't knock on the front door, did you? Did you change your mind? David——'

'I went to the store instead,' he said interrupting her harshly, and his face creased with some kind of pain. He saw her expression and continued angrily, 'Don't look at me like that! Of course I didn't know that your daughter was going to the store—how could I? I just went to the store and—and . . .' As Denise watched, he turned away from her and raked his hair, rumpling the dark glossy mass agitatedly. He said again, in low tones, 'How could I know? I couldn't.' He stopped and shook his head as if it hurt.

Denise was one of the few people in the world who had good cause not to scoff or disbelieve anything that might happen to her daughter, or be connected to Dana in any way. She asked him urgently, 'For God's sake, what happened? Did you see Dana? Did something happen to upset or frighten her in any way? How did you know to come back here?'

'I don't know!' he shouted, and something violent seethed inside him briefly, frighteningly and then was bottled up again and contained. He repeated, 'I just don't know. All I knew was that I had to come here. I—yes, something happened in town and it did upset Dana, but I don't really understand how—Mrs Haslow,' and he looked at her with a stunned expression overlaying the stress and emotion, 'your daughter wasn't in the store or anywhere else that I would know to look for her. But I walked around to the back of the store and found her anyway. I knew where she was. I knew she was in trouble.'

Denise stood quickly and walked over to him, tears filling her eyes. She touched him on the arm. 'Then do you think you could possibly find her and coax her out of whatever's got a hold of her?' she whispered. 'God, I'm so afraid of what might happen to her. Maybe we should both go out looking—maybe I should—should call somebody for help, oh, I don't know what to do!' And she broke into tears, wringing her hands futilely.

'No!' he said sharply, grabbing her by the shoulders. 'No, don't call anybody. I'll go out looking—she can't have gone far. I'll find her and bring her back safe. Just stay here, all right? It'll be . . .' and he hesitated before continuing, '. . . better if you're here calm and waiting for her. Look, are you okay? I really should leave.'

Reassured because she wanted to be reassured, Denise smiled and stepped back. It was a pitiful attempt at a smile, but it seemed to steady her. 'I'm fine, really. It's just—please, David, bring her back safe.'

He started to say something but stopped and just looked at her for a moment. Then, with another shake of his head as if to clear his mind, he left.

Sunlight glinting peacefully through deep green pines, making her half blind from the light. Dana blinked, and heard a far off, raucous call from a bluejay. Another bird answered. She smelled her own sweat, a faintly tangy scent, along with the fresh, aromatic smell of tree sap, along with rich earth. She was breathing hard as if she'd been in a race, panting.

Her eyes, drawn by the heavy weight of something in her hand, dropped, and shock coursed through every fibre of her being, along with the utter terror of not knowing how the gun got to be in her hand. A revolver! How did she get a hold of a revolver? What in Heaven's name was she doing with it? How had she got here, in the forest?

What, in God's name, was going on?

'Oh, no, no, no . . .' she whimpered, body shaking, mouth dry, muscles aching, as she thought back frantically, furiously over the immediate past. It was a smooth blank. What had she been doing? There was something that had upset her terribly, had got her so furious that she'd been shaking. What had happened?

Her eyes narrowed as memory clicked. Mick and the young girl. The nasty, sordid little scene behind the grocery store. Rage, fear, being threatened, and then . . . nothing. She couldn't remember, for the life of her, how she'd got the gun. How she'd got from there to here. What had happened to her. What she had done.

A total blank. She had blacked out and yet had apparently acted. She'd left her reality as she knew it and had travelled through something else. She'd fallen into the pit. She'd lost control. God knows where or

how she'd acquired the gun, and what she'd done with
it. She'd got the gun and then had run away. She was
on the run and trying to escape and—*Dear God, What
had she done?*

A moan of horror tumbled from her lips as she
stared at the gun in her hands, and yes, her hands, too,
as if it were all poison. Violence and then the gun, and
she couldn't remember. It was really true then. She
really was going crazy. It was sunlit and the world was
normal, but she was never going to be normal, had
never been normal in her life. And now she was in that
black pit and she was never going to get out again. She
was absolutely mad. It echoed in her mind, over and
over, and she wanted to scream at it to stop, but the
slam of reality was too immedite, too shocking, too
much to be ignored.

She'd wondered if she would be dangerous, if she
were ever to go crazy. The black gun in her right hand
blurred over as the sudden tears swam in her eyes.

She knew.

Suddenly she did scream, and a bird shot right up
into the air in a panic as her scream rolled over the
forest. She thought of that angry young man named
Mick; she thought of the terrified girl; she thought of
her mother; she thought of Mrs Simms, the grocer's
wife, of David, of Mrs Cessler. She thought of
everyone she loved, and she looked at that gun,
sobbing, so desperately afraid, and she slowly brought
it up, pointing it right at the pine tree's trunk.
Shaking, crying, and so sick at herself, she shot it until
all six bullet spaces had clicked. One empty click,
flinch, two, three, four ... Two shots, in rapid
succession, echoed through the forest, in the silence

after her scream. Two bullets, four empty spaces. Two bullets and four unremembered shots.

The self-disgust, the sweating fear, the panic and rage at herself, the self-hate became too much. She'd go home—no, she couldn't! *Oh, Mama, I don't want to hurt you! I'm sick, I'm sick——*

Dana's head jerked up as she heard a far-off shout. David. He was coming her way, his deep voice filled with desperation and sharp concern. He was calling her, had heard the shots. He couldn't find her. She couldn't face him, couldn't face anyone or anything else. Her head jerked back again as she looked at the gun and moaned again, flinging it at the tree in front of her. It landed with a dull thud. She suddenly wished she'd saved one of the bullets for herself.

She couldn't be allowed to hurt anyone else.

She started to run, pantingly, exhausted but making her legs work anyway, making them pump and drive, sending her up the slope. Running, she recognised where she was, and an intention fixed itself firmly in her mind. There would be no more pain, or loneliness, or numbing, nagging worry that she might again go into that black darkness.

'Dana!' David shouted. He was not far behind and gaining quickly. She was so tired. Her chest heaved and her face burned, and fire shot through her legs and chest. 'Dana, for God's sake! Stop a minute, let me talk to you——'

She shook her head, blindly. He must not catch her, must not stop her. It would be for the best.

'Dana, you're not by yourself in this! Just stop a moment and let me catch up with you, please!' His ragged voice was closer, and she could hear him running now. He was not far behind and catching up, but she was getting to the clearing at the top of the slope. She heard his words and wondered very fleetingly at how he'd known how lonely she felt, and then she was racing across the clearing to the cliff that plunged forty feet to rough, deadly rock. It would be enough.

'Dana, my God, don't do it!' David roared behind her, the bellow ripping out of him with the full force of his sudden, sharp, overwhelming realisation and stunned fear.

It cut through her own teeming emotions like a sharp knife, making her stumble as, not only the sound pierced her but the emotion itself, the fear knocking her over. But she'd picked herself up in an instant, and she could still make it if she pushed it and herself beyond the point of pain. She couldn't live with herself, she just couldn't.

At this point, her emotional crisis, the adrenalin flowing, her own awful decision—everything combined seemed to force her awareness into high gear. Her perception clicked over with an amazing rate of efficiency, recording every single instant of time, like frames from a movie, each movement, each gesture, each sound and sight being printed indelibly on her mind forever.

The sun was so very bright, and her legs quivered as she thrust up from the ground like a sprinter leaving the block, feet digging into the uneven ground for holds. The clearing seemed suddenly very small. Her chest heaved just one big, last breath and she held it. A drop of sweat had trickled into her mouth and she tasted salt. She had the mental image of something hugely powerful and incredibly fast being hurtled her way, at her back, and only looking back later could she realise that what she'd felt was David, bending all of his intellect and surging male body and screaming, protesting mind her way to halt her any way he could.

But for once in her life, Dana was so wrapped up in her emotions, she didn't heed his mental protest and she ran, so physically exhausted at this point that she was barely jogging instead of the sprint she'd tried for. She was just that much ahead of him. She hurtled herself, and the ground dropped from underneath her. Everything whirled and shifted and spinned, as she left the edge of the cliff, and her body twisted as she went over the edge. And the sunlight was so bright and beautiful, and the deep green, wonderfully graceful pines swaying in the wind, and the blue in the sky with the white from the clouds, and the brown earth and the smell of summer. She was going to remember it all, no matter what followed this life, and it would be the very last thing she knew of this life, that wonderful, majestic, aching beauty of this world . . .

. . . Something latched on to her wrist cruelly hard, manacling her like a band of iron, jerking her body up tight from that free, graceful last fall. Her body stopped short. She screamed in pain, from the lancing stab from her tortured, torn shoulder muscles, from her bruised body as it slammed stunningly into the side of the cliff. Something dark obstructed her yellow summer sun: David's head, hanging over the edge of the cliff, along with his long, tremendously strong arm and wrist and slim, quick, ruthless fingers. He was flat on his stomach, in one last ditch effort to stop her, and he'd somehow, incredibly, burst into that last moment of needed speed, throwing his body like a spear, leaping out full-length to snatch her wrist with an astonishing accuracy in aim.

Dana remembered thinking all that, as she hung between life and death, for several seconds just hanging in mid air, with the wind gusting behind her and cooling her, her shoulder practically torn from its socket, David's harsh, sobbing breathing sounding nearly in her ear. She thought about how terribly thin her wrist was, after all, and how the chances of him grabbing her right at that moment had been astronomically low, and how now she would not be able to escape the pit.

She heard him and felt him fighting for control over his straining body, only a few seconds ticking by since she'd tried to jump to her death. He was a very strong man and she was a comparatively small girl, weighing little. But bearing her full weight in such an abrupt jerk must have been excruciating for him as well as for her, and it took him a few moments to gather himself to the effort of dragging her back to safety at the top.

She heard his breathing as he took a deep breath, and then his shoulder muscle flexed and he started to pull her back slowly, inch by sweating, straining inch, and Dana felt herself being lifted inexorably up.

Overwrought, sobbing, immersed in the only true death-wish she'd ever experienced in her life, Dana clawed at his fingers and wrists, kicking convulsively against the cliff in an effort to get his hold to slip, drawing blood with her fingernails without realising, panting, 'No, let me go! Let me drop! Please, just let me die!'

He snarled out, 'Damn you, I will not! You aren't going to smash yourself to death, I won't have your blood on my conscience, too!'

She heard his strange words, the determination like iron that ran through his body, but he'd stopped pulling her up in spite of all the will in the world, for it was just impossible to drag her up when she struggled. His body weight was stretched out too far. They hung there, her wrist nearly broken by his white knuckled clamp on it. She had no feeling in that hand. 'I won't do it,' she gritted out, so exhausted and aching and so full of pain.

'Dana,' he panted, the hoarse sound not like him at all, something different and elemental, not a voice but a raspy whisper from the soul. It brought her head up and she stared into those dark eyes, now so desperate. Desperate for her sake. 'I can't bear to see you die, I can't. I can't bring you up. Your struggling. It's too much. You want to die, you can die. But I'll fall with you. I won't be left behind.'

Eyes already dilated from the strain of her emotion, Dana stared up at him and she saw the utter seriousness and implacability in him. She felt it. He was totally prepared to do it.

She made some kind of whimper, she didn't know what, and he suddenly shifted forward, bringing himself to the edge of the cliff, never lessening his grapple hold on her wrist. She felt herself shift downward a foot or so, a scraping slide against the rough jagged rock that lacerated her skin. 'I swear,' he whispered, 'I'll do it.'

At that keen point between life and death, where both met at the edge of the two sides of the coin, there was an utter stillness.

CHAPTER SIX

SHE flinched away at the thought of him dead, of that instant and vivid image of him broken and bleeding at the foot of the cliff, more so than she did at the thought of her own. 'No,' she gasped out raggedly, the physical strain on her body making her go limp, her own voice a mere thread of sound. 'No, don't! I'll come. Please, I'll come.'

A moment, as David panted and gathered up his strength, and then he started to pull again, and it was so excruciatingly painful for her as she felt muscles scream and threaten to tear, the rock catching at her bare arm and scraping it until it bled. David's harsh breathing and straining effort; and then she was grasping the top with her free hand; and then she was lying at the edge of the cliff, her hips and legs dangling; and then she was dragged totally back on to level ground.

Dana was suddenly crying as she fought for air, panting and gasping and shaking, the sobs uneven and a bare shudder of pitiful sound. David's hands shifted from under her arms to clasp her convulsively close, and she crept her own arms up and around his strong, sweating neck. She trembled and shook, and sobbed into his chest, and his arms held her tight as he trembled and shook. His face was in her hair, his hands moving across her back spasmodically, his strong frame shuddering over and over. Dana didn't know who was comforting whom. All she knew was that he was warm and real and immediate and caring, she felt that caring, and he knew how she'd felt and sympathised.

Her eyes were closed and her sobbing was dry, and she nuzzled him urgently in his neck, trying to hide her face in him and lose herself in him, and she felt his face moving in her hair and knew he was drowning his own sensations in her life, so imperiled a moment before and so safe now. Their entire heated bodies were intertwined and tangled as they sprawled on the hard ground, his legs hard and heavy against hers, his torso large and flat against her own chest, his hands thrust into the luxury of her long, thick, wind blown hair. His warm neck. She tasted his salt. Then her head was dragged back and his lips were brought to hers, shaking, fierce, clamping on her. He was drinking from her and slaking his fear and his thirst and his pent-up emotion, and she was kissing him back. Yet it wasn't quite what she would have, in her own vague and romantic daydreams, called kissing, but a biting, urgent, hurting, bruising reassurance of the other's life and living and safety and need.

Dana felt the sun pound down on her head, warming her exposed, bleeding arms and neck and the curve of her cheek as it was turned up. She felt the warmth of David's body as her skin melded to his, her arms thrown around him and holding him close, his own arms shuddering, crushing her, his weight half on her, half off. She could smell the pine and the grass and the summer aroma, mingled with David's own masculine scent. She heard his harsh, ragged breathing and someone else's—shocked to realise it was her own.

A rock dug into her hip. Yellow light blinded her and she couldn't see. The inside of his mouth was wet.

That was when the tears came, as he cradled her, and she let the drops fall hopelessly. Her own irreparably flawed person, the sweet breeze that delicately touched her heated skin, the man in front of her, now so gentle and caring, and that black, reeking pit she'd fallen into. It was worse than a prison. She was surrounded by the smells and sounds of freedom and sanity and goodness and healthiness, so that the knowledge of her own dark abnormality was more cruel than anything she'd ever imagined.

'Why didn't you let me die?' she whispered. Her eyes were closed now, her face hidden in him, and he held her head with one hand, the other arm wrapped so tightly around, she didn't think she could breathe, let alone move. His lips were moving over her forehead and temple, at the hairline, still reassuring himself of her living, hurting awareness.

'No. Oh, no.' It was spoken from the back of his throat, hoarsely.

'The gun,' she said, still shaking. 'The gun.' His hands passed over her, pressed her hard to him.

'Dana, everything is all right, I swear it. You're okay. You're going to be fine, just fine. I'm so sorry. I am so terribly sorry——' The muttered words barely reached her consciousness. She realised how tightly she'd been holding him to her, and loosened her grip slightly. She didn't think she could stand just yet.

She had to ask and didn't want to hear the answer, and whispered, mouth trembling, 'Did I hurt anyone?' The dull question had his head snapping up and he stared down at her, eyes widened, his head dark against that beautiful blue and white and yellow sky.

'You don't remember, then?' he asked her incredulously. 'You really don't recall any of it?'

Her face broke up. 'No! No, none of it. All I remember is standing against the wall behind the grocery store and seeing Mick come for me with his hands out as if he was going to grab at my neck. Then—then everything blanked out.' Her eyes, full of her fear and distress, pleaded mutely, as she asked stiffly, 'What happened to me, David? Where did I go?'

She could see that he was at a loss, and he appeared to search for words. Then he abruptly pulled her into a sitting position, his arms still wound around her, hard muscle digging into her back. He sighed. 'I think you have a lot to forgive me for, Dana. I think——' and his arms involuntarily tightened until she thought she would cry out from the pressure, '—I think that you somehow got tangled up in something that . . . came from me.' He paused, mouth open, trying to formulate words that just wouldn't come.

She said, sensing his discomfort, 'Like the nightmares.'

His head jerked. 'Like the nightmares.' His eyes narrowed on her, unsurprised. 'So you are aware of where they're coming from, then. I might have known. I had hoped—Lord, you're just something I'd never expected. I had thought that with a little more time, a little more discipline, I'd be able to control them, but it hasn't worked well, has it?'

'David, do you have a scar on your stomach?' She

leaned back against his arms comfortably, feeling the turbulent upheaval inside her subside.

He winced. 'You caught that nightmare, then, did you? How sensitive are you to them?'

Her eyes fell and she looked at the top button of his shirt, undone against the brown tanned skin. 'Just about as sensitive as I could get, I should think. Sometimes I have to check my stomach to make sure there isn't a scar there. It's—very disconcerting.'

'And have you been awakened by them?' He looked stunned and she couldn't blame him. Even when one intellectually accepted the face of psychic phenomena, it was an emotional jolt to be confronted with it.

'And haven't slept for the rest of the night, yes.' Her lips quivered into a smile that looked so wavering that he had to muffle a curse. Her eyes slid up quickly and this time there really was a slight smile in their depths. 'Cursing doesn't help much. It just sounds foul and doesn't change the situation.'

'Dana!' Looking considerably startled, his mouth thinned into a white line. 'You see too damned much for your own good. Are you able to read me this accurately all of the time, then?'

'No. It comes and goes. Sometimes your thoughts are very expressive. They leap at me, no matter how I try not to read them. Then I feel I've invaded your privacy, and—and——' Pale, she dropped her eyes and said dully, 'David, I really don't want this any more than you. I'm sorry. If I could turn it off, I would.'

'Sh. It's okay. I promise you, it will be all right.' This, she thought, even though she'd kept all of her distress and emotion out of her voice. He could read things too, after a fashion. His hand came up to stroke her hair. 'Would you like to know what I think happened earlier?'

She was unprepared for how her whole body trembled at his words. 'Oh, please. Yes, please.'

'When you ran from behind the store, you were . . . I think in a waking nightmare. I don't know how else to put it. You were caught in a memory of mine that you thought was real.'

He would have slowly and uncomfortably continued, but she halted him. 'Wait, what do you mean when I ran from behind the store? How did you know I was there? Were you there? I don't remember that.'

'I came to the back.' He fell silent, his eyes guarded and waiting. She sensed bewilderment. It was in tune with what she was feeling.

'Why did you do that? I know we didn't make enough noise for anyone to hear it from the front. I don't think anyone saw me go to the back. Why did you go to the back?' For some reason, she tensed as she waited for his answer.

'I don't know,' he said flatly. Then, as she continued to stare at him, more sharply, 'I don't know! I just knew that you were back there and that something was wrong.'

His arms fell away and he withdrew from her physically, but she barely noticed, not needing physical contact to have the sense of closeness, like many other people did. She wet dry lips. 'Why,' she asked slowly, needing to know badly, 'did you walk in to town today?'

His mouth thinned again into an ugly white line, tension making the two lines from nostrils to mouth more pronounced, the furrow between his brows deep. His eyes darkened, his brown hair blown all out of tidiness, and that stern, tense look made him appear suddenly very dangerous. But Dana didn't see that in him; she saw more with her mind and sensed his anger stemming from bewilderment and confusion.

'I was looking for you,' he said shortly, setting his teeth together with a snap. Dana didn't heed the warning, clenching her hands into fists.

'But why to town? Why not stop at the house, or did you?' she persisted. 'But no, you must have arrived on the scene too soon to have stopped at the house. Why to town? How did you know I was there?'

'It was a guess.' His powerful shoulders hunched.

'Don't lie to me, David. Of all people, not me.'

'I couldn't know!' he ground out. 'I just needed to walk off some tension——'

'You knew.'

'I thought I'd look out for you. I thought we could have that talk——'

'You felt something building in yourself. You were afraid.'

'I was afraid of nothing!'

'You sensed me.' It was uttered with complete certainty.

'*How in God's name could I?*' he thundered, and this time she felt the danger in him palpably, and she wasn't sure if the wave of fear came from herself or from him.

'Don't!' she screamed, clenching her hands at her temples. Moaning at the onslaught of anger and bafflement he exuded, she started to pound her fists at her temples, concentrating on the physical pain instead of the emotional.

'Stop that!' He grabbed her hands and forced them down, away from her. He glared down at her bent head. 'Why are you so intent on hurting yourself?'

'I hate it!' she threw at him. 'I hate myself, I hate this, I hate you! Get out of my head! Don't you know what you're doing to me? Can't you feel it? Will you stop *lying* to yourself?'

A moment of silence. Birds crying out, diving overhead, sun shining benignly, breeze rustling. He stared at her, eyes wide. 'I sensed you,' he whispered, the admission coming from dry lips. 'I don't know how, but I sensed you.'

She closed her eyes, trembling in the way she knew he'd never let himself. 'And I'm as big a liar as any of them. I don't hate you. I don't—don't want to die. I— I——' She couldn't finish. A tear dripped down her cheek.

'Dana.' It was gentle; he was so very gentle. 'You know I'm afraid, too.'

And she was back in his arms, clinging. They stayed like that for a long, long time.

Back at the house, David opened up the back door quietly and let Dana precede inside. They found Dana's mother sitting straight and pale at the kitchen table, an undrunk cup of coffee in front of her. Her head snapped up and relief came into her eyes as she stood to wordlessly clasp Dana close to her. Dana briefly put her head on her mother's shoulder, slumping against her for a moment and feeling nothing but a vast relief to be back within the setting of normality.

Then her mother stepped back and surveyed both of their faces, noting strain. 'Is everything all right, then?' she asked quietly, eyes lingering on David's dark visage.

He smiled slightly at her, the lines at his mouth more pronounced. 'We have a lot to talk about, Mrs Haslow.' She nodded without surprise, her glance flickering back to Dana, who sat down heavily. 'And both Dana and I think that we should get something settled right here and now.' At the question in her eyes, he again smiled and produced the black revolver for her perusal.

'Oh, thank God!' She took it gingerly, and then said feelingly, 'I've always felt nervous about having this around, but then Jerry insisted. The first thing I'm going to do is get rid of it for good!' She disappeared down the hall, leaving Dana smiling without amusement. David leaned against the counter, arms crossed.

'I really must have frightened her to death. What in the world did I do?' she asked him. 'You never said.'

Something violent quivered in the air for a moment and then whisked away. His eyes were dark. 'You frightened us both,' was his only immediate reply. Dana's heart sank.

Her voice shook. 'Why won't you tell me? Is it so horrible, then?'

'No! No, it isn't.' He was then right beside her and stroking her face with long, calloused fingers, which only served to make her shake even more. 'It's just—hard for me. I think we'd better wait until your mother is back here.'

'Well, I'm back.' The voice came composedly from the doorway. David's hand fell slowly away. Dana jerked in her seat. Denise gave her daughter a strange look, which Dana didn't catch, as she was staring fixedly down at her clasped hands. 'What was it you wanted to talk about? I somehow get the impression that you know more about this than even Dana.' Denise moved on into the kitchen. 'Would either of you like coffee?'

Both answered together, 'Please.' And they looked at each other, David acutely uncomfortable, Dana abashed. Denise's brows went up.

Dana watched while her mother poured two cups, suddenly aware of how empty she was. She was beginning to feel the consequences of her lack of appetite, along with the emotional stress of the last few hours. She felt strung out, trembly. Denise spoke over her shoulder. 'One thing I've learned over the years, David, is that you never take what seems to be coincidental circumstance for granted around Dana. Here you are.' She handed him a cup and he poured milk into it and gave it wordlessly to Dana. She took it as silently, and then realised that her mother was watching them oddly. Denise handed him another cup, for which he thanked her and sipped at as she sat back at the table. She asked quietly, 'Whose story goes first, or are they both so intertwined it's the same story?'

Again David looked at Dana as she lifted her eyes to meet his. His face was inscrutable. She could feel how inwardly tense and uncomfortable he felt. More used to talking to her mother about this, Dana took a deep breath and replied, 'We are having the same nightmares, Mom. They're his——'

He said very quietly, '. . . memories, Mrs Haslow. They're memories of Vietnam.' His chin was sunk on to his chest as he watched them both from under heavy, straight brows. Denise audibly sucked in her breath. 'For some reason Dana is extremely sensitive to me and is picking up these . . .'

'—emotions,' Dana supplied as he hesitated. His eyes flickered back to her. There was disconcertment in his eyes. She sympathised, she really did. He wasn't quite used to her yet. Denise had also swivelled her head to Dana, eyes wide. 'And you know how I can't control this, Mom. So while David can somehow clamp down on his control hard enough for his own— stability, I'm left wide open to them and can't.'

'Stability is not quite the word for it,' David said heavily, sighing. 'But you'll get the picture.' Dana wasn't quite sure to whom he was talking, her mother or herself. 'Dana doesn't remember what happened today. But what I think happened was that she was somehow caught in—for lack of a better term right now—a waking nightmare somehow. She was involved in an unpleasant scene downtown, which, by the way, I still don't know everything about.' He looked down at Dana, brows raised.

'Mick was being nasty to a young girl,' she said briefly in explanation. 'I caught her distress and went back to see if I could help her.'

'I see. Well,' David's low, pleasant voice paused as he searched for words. 'Apparently, I somehow knew from either Dana or myself that something was about to happen, and I came on the scene just in time to see Dana hit Mick and run. I stayed just for a moment or so, just long enough to confront the boy, and then I came right after her.' He turned to Dana and walked across the room to her, leaning against the table, very near. She listened, body still slightly shaking. 'You ran

back here, made up a bundle of medical supplies, and
got your father's gun from the study as your mother
and I came upon you. From things that you said, I
think you were involved somehow in—God, this is
incredible—something that happened to me in
Vietnam. You appeared to actually be living through
it, yourself.' Despite all his control and deliberately
calm voice, something ragged ran through it. Denise
made a sound but neither David nor Dana paid any
attention to her. 'I was,' he said painfully, 'a helicopter
pilot in 'Nam. I flew wounded men to MASH units,
and sometimes supplies, so I was near quite a bit of
the fighting . . .'

Pain lanced through Dana's head and she cried out,
leaning forward to put her head on the table. The
headache was like a physical blow, pounding at her
temple. 'I crashed!' she sobbed out dryly. 'Oh, I'm so
dizzy . . .'

A hard warm hand descended to her shoulder for
support and she vaguely heard David's exhalation of
air as he felt her pain, too. He put a hand to his
forehead, clamping down hard on himself. She could
feel it, like a tight band across her chest. He was
pushing himself under a rigid control again. Her
muscles tensed. She was getting hotter and hotter.
Sweat trickled down the side of her neck. 'I crashed,'
he repeated harshly. 'Someone had fired on the
helicopter as I was making a trip out for a few men
who caught some sniper fire. Their unit leader had
taken the rest of the men out to pursue the Viet Cong.
They'd been apparently killed, ambushed. My engine
was hit and I went down in the forest.'

'My head, my head,' Dana moaned, the pain

throbbing. 'I hit my head. It's so hot. They aren't men, they're boys, and they're going to die! Without me, they'll die!' Someone was shouting at her and it took a while for the words to penetrate. As she heard David, she slowly opened her eyes and found him standing over her.

'Snap out of it, Dana!' he snapped urgently. 'You'll drive us both crazy! Snap out of it, for God's sake!' She saw, as she looked at him, how he then realised that she had some measure of sanity in her eyes again. He was breathing hard. Sweat stood out on his collar-bone, glistening on the brownness. His firm mouth was distorted into an ugly twist as he fought down his memories. 'Don't go back. They died, Dana. All of them died. Don't go back! God, I can't—I can block myself, but I can't block out you. Don't, please. It's over, do you hear?'

As she looked up into his contorted, pain-filled eyes, her own blurred with tears and her face crumpled. 'All of them?' she asked brokenly. 'Everyone died?' She heard a hiss from her mother.

'All of them,' he replied, more quietly, attempting gentleness. 'They'd been killed. A band of the Vietnamese found them and slit their throats. There was nothing anybody could have done.'

'All five,' she whispered.

'All five.' His fingers on her shoulders tightened and he then let go, squatting in front of her chair, still close. She was looking down at him, could see his upturned, strong jawline, the line of his throat that looked at once so strongly corded and yet so vulnerable as she caught a pulse beating on the side. She saw him breathe deeply, the movement heaving

his chest, the way his shirt tapered down to his flat
stomach.

'Was that when you got hurt?' she asked numbly.
'Was that when you were wounded and left for dead?'

'My dear Lord,' Denise said quietly.

'Yes,' David said baldly. His corded hands clasped
hers.

'The nightmares are real. You are scared, aren't
you?' Suddenly needing to see for herself, she reached
out and pulled his shirt up abruptly, never considering
the intimacy of the act, never even thinking of being
embarrassed at her own audacity, never even dreaming
that he could possibly be offended by such an action.

'Dana!' her mother protested this in a shocked tone
of voice, but again neither of them heeded her.

David simply knelt on the floor from his squatting
position, holding his powerfully muscled torso straight,
arms to his sides. His eyes told her that he understood
her need, and she unbuttoned his shirt with trembling
fingers, yanking it wide open. Her hands clenched into
fists, crumpling the material, and then fell to her lap as
she stared at his dark brown chest, a sprinkle of silky
black hair at the top of his rib cage that arrowed down
to disappear into his jeans. The skin was smooth, hard
from the muscle underneath but silken to the touch,
she found, as her fingertips touched his stomach,
shaking more violently as she traced the outline of a
white, old scar, a thick mar against the perfection of
his tan. He held himself there, steady and still. In spite
of herself, Denise shifted also to look, fascinated.
Dana's eyes, huge in her pinched face, slowly rose to
meet his, and he nodded.

'It's real. It really is real. I'm not crazy. The knife.'

Her hand knotted and she unconsciously shoved it
into her own stomach, reminiscent of his own action,
thirteen years ago. Her face twisted briefly into agony.
Darkness swirled like a whirlpool and her mother
cried out as Dana silently pitched forward. David
jerked out his arms and caught her before she'd
slumped to the floor.

He knelt there a moment, his arms wrapped around
Dana's still, slight body, her head on his naked, warm
chest. She was utterly limp. He bent his head to look
at her face and saw her eyes closed, and he buried his
face for a moment with a deep tired sigh into her thick
hair. His shoulders were dejectedly slumped. Then,
very carefully, he shifted her in his arms to pick her
up. Her head fell back on his arm in an alarmingly
lifeless manner, exposing the long, slender, vulnerable
curve to her pale neck. 'She's all right, Mrs Haslow,'
he murmured softly as Denise came around the table
quickly, her face worried. He looked at the blue vein
under her white translucent skin at the side of her
neck. Unbidden, the thought that this was the perfect
place for a killing stroke came to his mind, followed by
an immediate surge of protectiveness for her, along
with a sense of anger at himself and the memories he
couldn't let lie. 'She just fainted. She's had a hard
ordeal today, and my guess is on little food. Where can
I put her?'

He followed Dana's mother up the stairs and in to
Dana's room, putting her very carefully down on the
neatly made bed before looking around him. He bent
and checked her pulse at her slim, bruised wrist and
found it steady. He frowned at the bruises and then
winced at the evidence of Dana's earlier deadly

intention. Then he sat down gingerly on the edge of
the bed and stared down at the still face in front of
him. It was only as he saw her without any sign of
stress or guard on her face that he realised just how
nicely proportioned her features were. Dana was, he
discovered, quite beautiful. He said to Denise as she
moved to the other side of the bed and looked down at
her daughter, 'I think it would be best, under the
circumstances, if I were to leave the area. I think Dana
would be better off. She'd be safe.' As he said this, he
was surprised to find how hard the words were to say.

'Would she?' Denise said oddly. She passed a gentle
hand over Dana's still, white cheek. 'Perhaps if you
would sit with her for a little while, I could go and fix
us all something to eat. Dana hasn't had much in her
stomach, and I'm sure it will help steady her when she
wakens.'

David turned his head to look at Denise sharply, his
mouth opened to say something. She met his stare
calmly, her own face as lined with stress as either of
theirs. He closed his mouth and silently nodded. She
left the room.

Dana started to swim up to consciousness sluggishly,
the blackness receding to grey and then daylight as she
reluctantly opened her eyes. She was on something
soft and turned her head as she also registered warmth
from one of her hands. David was sitting on her bed,
cradling her slim hand between his two. 'That was
stupid of me, wasn't it?' she murmured, grinning a
lopsided, rueful grin.

He didn't smile. 'No. You'd put up with a lot, I'd
say. It was entirely understandable.'

She unconsciously began to tense, but he leaned

forward and stroked one hand over her forehead and down the side of her face. She whispered, 'What is it?' Her eyes searched his face.

'I can't keep anything to myself around you,' he said irritably, and she flinched. 'I'm sorry, Dana. I didn't mean that the way it sounded, but—damn, girl, you have to realise how unsettling this is.'

Immensely tired, she turned her head away and nodded as she stared at the other wall. The bed creaked as David moved, and then his hands fastened on her shoulders and pulled her up to a sitting position abruptly. She winced at the pain in her sore shoulder, surprised at his unexpected and unsensed action, and then one of his hands was dragging her hair and gripping the back of her neck to force her head around. She stared at him with wide eyes as her heart started to pound, and his head moved down, his mouth covering hers.

She kissed his warm, searching lips almost involuntarily, her own mouth falling open as her eyes closed and her arms went around his neck. His own arms wrapped around her so tightly, hard against his chest, that she felt her breath being forced out of her. Then he let her go and she fell back on to her pillow, stunned at her own feelings and the unexpectedness of the whole thing.

'Dana, I'm going away,' he said harshly. 'I'm going to re-lease Grace's house and move. I can't go on living here, knowing I'm the cause of all your strain and trouble! This can't continue the way it is and we both know it! You're too thin, you aren't eating, and somehow you're making me open and vulnerable to all of those memories I'm working so hard to bury. It's best for all of us. I'll leave as soon as I can.'

Dana had barely enough time to register what he was saying before the shock hit her. Her eyes fell away and she nearly gasped at the dismay that she felt over his words, surprised that she should care so much. But she did. She cared very much whether she saw him again or not, even though she knew he was the cause of so much of her distress lately. She cared a great deal, altogether too much.

CHAPTER SEVEN

'It won't work,' she found herself saying dully. Silence stretched out in the room and she rolled her head on the pillow to look at David, her eyes as dull as her voice. 'It won't work,' she repeated, at his frowning stare. 'Do you remember what Mrs Cessler told you about what happened when my father died? I felt it, David. I felt it as if it were my own. He wasn't anywhere near me at the time. Do you really think that you would change things by leaving? You wouldn't. If I'm as sensitive to you right now, I know that it won't matter where you are. I'll still feel your pain.'

Absolutely nothing showed on David's face, and yet she felt the despair hit him as if she'd physically attacked him, and she winced. 'God, why me?' he burst out, half roaring it in his frustration. 'Why me? Why the hell did you have to get involved? Why can't you get free of this, damn it?'

She put up both hands, hiding her face from him. 'Do you really think I want this?' she gritted, digging the heels of her hands into her eyes, seeing blind white sparks from the pressure. 'Don't you think that if I could cut that part out of me with a knife, I would? I should have died this afternoon, I should have died!'

'Don't say that! Shut up!' A hiss of breath, a glare, hands clenched. She didn't look at him.

Then, she brought her hands down slowly and stared at him, hard. 'Besides,' she said softly, 'aren't you as trapped as I am? Because you can never get away from yourself, your memories, no matter how you try. You suppress it and you suppress it, but it always bursts out of you somehow. A nightmare, a sleepless night. A lonely and isolated life. If you could cut that out of you, you would.'

He stood, a violent movement, stalking through the room turning. Though he opened his mouth to say something, nothing came out. They stared at each other, both tense, as the afternoon sun threw a mottled pattern through the curtains, over them both.

Dana was the first to turn as her mother walked into the room, glancing at them both with eyebrows slightly raised. She smiled at her mother, noting the lines still on her face, the greying hair, the fan of wrinkles at her eyes. Denise said quietly, 'I thought that you would know when I was through fixing the meal, Dana. You always do. It's ready downstairs, if you are.' And she looked again at David. He was staring out of the window, his back rigid.

'I'll come down with you now, Mom,' Dana said quickly, not looking towards the window. 'I'm sure that David will want to wash up.'

It sounded flimsy and they all knew it, but her mother accepted her words without question, and they went downstairs to the empty kitchen.

Sitting down to the simple meal, Dana ate without saying anything as she thought about the man who was upstairs in her room. She was startled into jumping when her mother spoke.

'Dana.' She looked up. Denise was looking at her so strangely, and she lifted a brow in question. 'Do you realise that you haven't been sensing me at all today?'

Dana's face went blank. 'W-what do you mean?'

'You know very well what I mean.' Denise studied her consideringly, greying head cocked to one side. Dana flushed and her eyes fell away. 'You have always known when to come down to the supper table. I've never in my life had to call you. And yet, for some reason and for the first time in your life, you didn't know to come down tonight. Why is that, do you suppose?'

Looking down at her half-eaten meal, Dana mumbled in a shaking voice, 'I don't know.' Suddenly panicked, she reached out with her mind almost desperately, unsure as to how to do something that had always been second nature to her. She relaxed when she could feel her mother's quiet, accepting, questioning mind. She said more steadily, 'I don't know. I can feel you there now.'

'But what I'm wondering is why you couldn't feel me then?' They stared at each other, and then Dana turned before the footsteps sounded at the doorway.

David appeared there, wide shoulders filling the space, contrasting with lean hips. His hair was ruffled as if he had run his fingers through it, and his face was tired. He moved slowly, as if he were an old man. Dana knew a surge of tenderness and very nearly stood to go to him. At the doorway he paused, and his eyes ran over them both briefly. 'If you don't mind, I think that I'll be leaving now,' he said remotely. 'I have several things that I need to do.'

Dana didn't respond as she looked at him, eyes wide, trying with all of her might to sense what he was feeling and thinking. Denise said immediately, 'Of course, by all means, don't feel like you have to stay. You've been such a help to us already today. I don't know what we would have done without you.'

David just looked at her, his expression sardonic, making Dana flush painfully for both him and herself. Then without a backward glance, he strode to the door and left. Dana was left with a bereft, bewildered emotion gnawing at her chest, unable to sense his purpose or to untangle her own mixed emotions.

The next day was very quiet. Dana spent her time indoors, either reading listlessly, sleeping fitfully in the afternoon, or working halfheartedly at her needlepoint. She felt exhausted, drained, hollowed out. When she mentioned this to her mother, Denise merely replied that she wasn't surprised, considering how emotion-filled and tense the earlier day had been. Dana sighed, knowing that her mother was right, and yet at the same time feeling impatient with herself and the world around her. Everything seemed curiously empty to her. Occasionally, out of sheer loneliness and boredom, she could consciously reach out with her questing mind to reassure herself of her mother's presence. She was puzzled and uncertain as to why she was not constantly attuned to her parent as she'd always been in the past, and she was afraid to ask why.

The evening stretched out endlessly, and she was more than ready to make her way up to her room at the end of it, tired, and oddly close to tears. She dropped into a deep sleep almost immediately.

Everything was blackness. She'd never seen such a black night in her life. It was hot, it was muggy, it was so stifling and horribly quiet that she thought she might go out of her mind with it. The worst was the tiny shuffling, grunting noises in the dark of the night, for though she couldn't see what was going on, she could hear, and she knew, oh, she knew what was happening.

They were piling the dead. After taking as many of the soldiers out as possible, she/he had returned to make sure there was no one left after the terrible skirmish between the soldiers and the Vietnamese from the small village. Rage filled her/him at the very thought of the soldiers ordered to shoot on the nearly defenceless villagers who were armed with ancient muskets, pitchforks, knives and other farm implements. The soldiers were sick at heart, the villagers sick with fear, and the whole night reeked with the stench of the fear and the sickness.

It suddenly reeked with something else, too. As her/his nostrils quivered at the unexpected smell of gasoline, something flared to her/his right, unbelievably bright and glaring, and her/his head automatically turned in that direction, hand thrown up against the bright shock to his senses. And he gave a great shout of rage and horror as he saw what was burning.

They were burning the dead villagers. He had never seen anything so utterly horrible in his life.

Screams echoed from the edges of the forest where the surviving villagers had taken refuge, and he gradually became aware that his own shouting had never ceased. His shouting was a scream, too.

Everything became suddenly, intensely hot, and Dana bolted stark upright in her bed, wetness trickling off her entire body, the echoes of her own horrified screams still reverberating through her room and the dark, silent house. Still in the grip of the horrible scene she had just dreamt, she scrambled out of bed and lurched for the bathroom, her hand clamped over her shaking mouth. There she was wretchedly sick, the vivid memory of the sights and the smells making her retch painfully. Her hands were shaking and she was hicupping in deep, dry sobs. Something burst into the bathroom and her mother switched on the light, sleepy, confused, asking in a ragged voice, 'Dana? Oh, honey, are you all right?'

She didn't bother to answer, stumbling back to her room and throwing on her bathrobe as fast as her two shaking, weak hands would let her. It was not very quick. Then, stumbling from the shock of the nightmare, the rude awakening, and her own sick reaction, she made her way to the head of the stairs and crept down them, hanging on to the banister. Her limbs were shaking so.

Her mother followed her to the head of the stairs, asking in a fear-sharpened voice, 'Dana? Answer me! Dana, are you all right?'

Dana never turned, intent on one thing only.

She was out of the door and into the night, half falling down the porch steps, and then something large and hard came out of the black and still night, wrapping two strong arms roughly around her quaking body so tightly she couldn't breathe, and the shock of the bodily impact, along with the utter and immense comfort of the knowledge of just who it was that held her made Dana really cry noisily. She tried to talk to him through her tears, unintelligibly.

David was holding her, soothing her, brushing the hair off of her hot forehead as he muttered into her ear things that she never really deciphered. She just clutched at him and shook as she tried to tell him about her horror and the terrible images that still clung like sticky cobwebs to her mind.

'I know. I know. Hush, I know.' He repeated the monotonous wording in a half croon until it sank into her mind.

Then a strange voice, also male, impinged on her consciousness as someone nearby said deeply, 'Dear Heaven, it really is true.'

Dana had her face buried in the bare warmth of David's heaving chest, her salty tears wetting them both, making her cheek slide along the silky hardness of his collarbone. She felt his hand at the back of her head as he held her against him, his face against her hair, her ribs aching from the pressure of his arms crushing her.

He said finally, 'Come on. Let's go inside. Come on, Dana. We'll go in and just sit on the couch a while, until you're feeling better. That's it, just put one foot in front of the other and move your legs. It's not so hard, is it?'

He was more than half supporting her, though she was able to lift her streaked face away from his shoulder as they slowly walked up the porch steps into the now lit house, her worried mother standing by the front door and the strange man following behind. She was beginning to calm down now, but only as she felt the reverberations of David's own internal upheaval begin to subside. He had his arm tightly around her slim shoulders. She felt him heave a great sigh as if he were straining under a huge load.

Dana sank down to the couch as her legs gave way, and she drew the edges of her bathrobe together self-consciously as the strange man looked at her thoughtfully. She returned his stare almost defiantly. He was older than David, somewhere in his forties, and his greying hair was black at the back. His face was heavily lined, and his eyes, as she looked closer seemed full of compassion.

Someone sat down beside her: David. She didn't turn her head. Denise, understandably bewildered at the unexpected entrance of not one, but two men and one of them a stranger, came into the room and closed the door behind her. Dana's eyes went to her, and she asked her daughter for the fourth time, quietly now, 'Are you going to be all right, dear?'

It was a very, very tired one, but it was a smile nevertheless, and as she smiled at her mother, she nodded. She watched as Denise moved to a seat and sank into it, belting her own robe firmly about her thickening waist.

Then the stranger spoke, and Dana looked at him instead. 'You are Dana?' he asked her pleasantly, as if being awakened out of a sound sleep at two thirty in the morning was an everyday occurrence for him, and so indeed it seemed since he was the only one of the four of them who was more or less dressed. Then Dana looked down at his feet, randomly, and found that he was barefoot like the rest of them, which for some reason made her feel slightly more at ease.

She nodded silently, her face in the warmth of the golden living-room light pale, and her features wary, tense. Strain was etched on her face, shown in the pinched skin and her huge, dilated eyes that seemed just a shade too bright. Her hand tightened convulsively at the throat of her robe.

David said quietly, 'I'd like for you both to meet a friend of mine, Peter Cartwright. This is Dana's mother, Denise Haslow.'

Dana bent her head as she heard her mother murmur some sort of greeting, and the man's pleasant reply. She found herself trying to grope out with her mind in order to somehow read this stranger's character, and to her own discomfort found that she couldn't. This man was to her about as readable as a brick wall. She withdrew into herself almost physically, eyes shuttered, legs close together and shoulders hunched.

Then David was speaking again. 'You had the nightmare too.' It was a statement of fact and no question, but she found herself nodding in affirmation anyway. Her eyes slid up and she found Peter Cartwright's keen gaze on her. She slid her gaze evasively back to the floor and she patiently started to count the threads in the coarse carpet shag at her feet. She wondered why this man was making her feel so self-conscious. 'Peter,' David was saying to her mother, 'is staying with me for a while and had a bit of a rude awakening, as I know you did. Please forgive me for that.'

'Good Heavens!' Denise expostulated. 'It's not your fault, David! After all, none of this would have happened if Dana——' She faltered as Dana threw up her head and glared at her quite pointedly, then glanced at Peter. Dana didn't know why she even bothered. She had the awful feeling it was too late. She looked unwillingly at David, fully aware that he had seen her rather obvious hint and half afraid that he would be offended or angry at it.

But David was looking at her very hard and very seriously, as if trying to convey something to her without words, and as this dawned on her and as she

futilely tried to make-believe that everything was all
right, he was saying something that made her whiten
at the betrayal of confidence. It was a sinking, terrible
feeling, and becoming familiar. It was how she'd felt
when she had heard of Mrs Cessler's betrayal.

'I've taken the liberty of telling Peter something
about the nature of what you and I are—experiencing
right at the moment,' he said quietly. 'He'd like to
help us try to work out our——'

'What did you tell him?' she burst out, feeling
utterly naked and alone.

He hesitated. 'Quite a bit,' he finally admitted, and
jerked slightly as she flashed out her accusation.

'Liar! You told him everything, didn't you? Don't
think I don't know it! How could you do this to me? I
trusted you!' And everyone started to talk at once,
which was more than she could handle. The easy tears
welled up and she stared at the blurred, still image of
the man who sat so close to her. There was a world of
condemnation and hurt in her eyes. 'It wasn't yours to
tell!' she whispered shakingly, and jumped up to run
out of the room. She pelted down the hall and bolted
into the first haven she came to, which happened to be
her father's study.

Rapid, heavy footsteps followed her, and she
searched hopelessly for a lock that had never been
there, feeling terribly invaded. They stopped abruptly,
and she could distinguish two low, intense voices,
arguing, one of them Peter's, one David's. She sagged
against the door, so very tired and so very tense, and
she heard something harsh in David's voice. Then
someone walked away from the other side, and she
drew in a deep, unsteady breath.

It had been David walking away. And footsteps were continuing to stop just outside her door. She unconsciously braced her shoulder against the wood and winced as it was her sore one. She then collapsed at the innocuous sound of his voice, sounding utterly normal as it penetrated the wood barrier.

'Dana, I know that you're feeling betrayed by David's actions, but I'd like to assure you that he did only what he thought would be healthy for both you and him.' The older man paused. She remained silent, not rejecting his overtures and not acknowledging them either. He continued, his voice utterly calm and pleasant, and in spite of herself she found that she was relaxing. 'I was in 'Nam when David was. That was how we met. He was, as you already know, a helicopter pilot, and I was a doctor just out of medical school. Please, may I come in and talk with you?'

She hesitated and very nearly said no. She was so close to saying no that she had her mouth open and her lips forming the small word. But even as she was preparing in her mind that negative response, she found her hands coming out and slowly turning the knob and opening the door. She peered around the edge of it at the older man, her face wary, ready to bolt again at the slightest provocation. He didn't move but merely smiled at her, so very kindly and gently that she found herself moving back from the door and he came into the room, shutting the door behind him.

'I'd like to tell you a little bit about David, if I may?' Peter said, cocking an inquisitive eyebrow at her. It was probably the best thing he ever could have said to her, and she found herself nodding almost immediately. She watched as he settled himself against

the old oak desk and smilingly invited her to sit down
in the comfortable seat in front of him. She complied,
rubbing at her temples at a slight nagging pain there,
and listened patiently as he started to talk. 'David has
always been a very strong personality. He's determined, aggressive, and forceful when he chooses to be.
When we were in 'Nam, I can remember his baffled
rage at the whole chaotic upheaval there, the guerrilla
warfare, the killing of innocent villagers by both
sides . . .' She flinched violently, but he didn't seem to
notice as he continued, '. . . everything about 'Nam
was an intense, bizarre experience that young men
barely out of boyhood were thrust into, and were
expected to be killers. David was the kind of person
that had a very great respect for human life, and the
terrible waste of it in 'Nam was something utterly
alien to his personality.

'Oh, 'Nam was something that David hadn't been
prepared for. None of us had been. None of us really
knew what to expect, what was going on. The
government said that we were to go and fight for
justice, and so we all went, with one idea or another of
what it would be like. Many of the kids had been
raised on John Wayne movies, and they had
envisioned themselves becoming great heroes. David
and I were, in our different professions, only
interested in trying to prevent the loss of human life,
futilely so, sometimes, in the middle of a crazy world
and a half understood war. And no matter how many
we could congratulate ourselves on saving, there were
still so many who died.

'So you can see perhaps, through what I'm trying to
tell you and through your own experiences with

David, just what had happened to him in that
relatively brief time overseas. Futility, rage, horror, all
of those feelings were thrust upon him, so to speak.
David is a survivor, and one of his survival tactics in
'Nam had been a peculiar ability to block himself up
tightly in what I term a "little black box". He kept his
emotions on a very tight rein; he simply refused to let
go of his control and lose touch with reality, like many
of the kids did. He held on grimly to both himself and
the reality of himself. I really think it was one of the
main things that got him through the nightmare. But
now he's left holding on, with old feelings that should
have been let out as soon as it was safe to do so, and
they are now spilling out, intense and frightening.
Dana, I'd like to thank you, because you are the reason
for David finally coming out and saying that he
needed to talk to someone about 'Nam, to let it out
and finally exorcise the ghost. You frightened him into
it, and if it hadn't been for you, he might have held all
of it in until it destroyed him. When it was just
himself who was suffering, he was able to keep it in
and stay silent; we are always willing to damage
ourselves more than any other. And what you've done
is to make him ready to save himself, in order to save
another.'

Dana looked down at her hands. With her head bent
and her chestnut hair falling forward, the curve of her
neck seemed very fragile and her fingers, though
tightly clasped, trembled.

Peter said quietly, very kindly, 'And I think it's
time we called tonight quits, for it is very late. I just
couldn't let you go tonight without trying just a
little to get you to see David's dilemma, and why he

chose to tell me perhaps more than was comfortable for you.'

She cleared her throat and said, 'You're a psychiatrist, aren't you?'

A slight hesitation and then softly, 'Yes, I am. I hope that doesn't frighten you away from me. I'd like to talk to you some more, perhaps tomorrow, if you wouldn't mind.'

She took a deep breath, held it, and slowly eased it out, giving in to the release of tension. 'I think I'd like that.'

His answering smile was in his eyes. 'Good. Thanks for listening.'

When they walked into the lit kitchen, they found Denise and David sitting silently at the table, both with coffee in front of them, both brooding. At their entrance, Denise jumped up and glanced quickly from Peter to Dana, but Dana was watching only David. He didn't look up at all. His hands tightened on his coffee cup, and his face, shuttered and withdrawn, was turned to the window where the first grey streaks of the predawn were filtering through. His strong shoulders were hunched.

She walked over and stood beside his chair and still he didn't look up. Uncertain as to what she should do or how she should do it, she slowly raised a hand and held it briefly in the air before dropping it lightly on to his shoulder and squeezing with her fingers. He stayed immobile, walled into himself, and finally in desperation she tried to convey to him a strong welling of reassurance in silence, pushing it at him with all of her mental capacity. His shoulder muscles relaxed, slumped, and he sighed, passing a large hand over his eyes tiredly. Then he looked up at her, weary, impassive. She smiled. She'd felt his troubled mind ease.

Exhaustion then hit her like a ton of bricks and she slumped slightly where she stood, vaguely aware of her mother and Peter talking in low voices at the other end of the room. David stood quickly and passed a supporting arm around her shoulders, steering her to the hallway. Feeling suddenly embarrassed at the intimacy of the movement, she dragged her feet and glanced back at her mother, but Denise was intent on whatever Peter was telling her, her own face lined with signs of weariness. Dana looked at David and surprised a smile of understanding on his face. But nevertheless, he still impelled her to the staircase. She gave in.

Back in her room, she dropped her bathrobe on the floor uncaringly and sank down to her bed, slumping against the bedpost. The bed creaked as David eased himself on to it also, close beside her, his denim clad thigh touching hers.

'What did Peter tell you?' he asked quietly.

She looked at him. 'You know.'

'No, I don't,' he replied, and she felt a wave of anger at him. His brows shot up.

'You do,' she returned flatly. 'You know you do. Why are you trying to hide from yourself? Why aren't you acknowledging that part of you that is, for some reason God only knows, sensitive to me? You're not only lying to yourself, you're trying to lie to me, and it doesn't work. You can't pull that one off.'

He surged to his feet, prowled around the room, turned. 'I'm *not* you!' he grated, and she flinched. 'I'm *not* used to this, I haven't been attuned to this all my life like you have! You moan and complain, and you say that you have this great affliction! Just how would you feel if you suddenly lost that "great affliction" forever? How would you feel if that part of you was well and truly silenced?'

She blanched, became incredibly white, her mouth shaking. He may try to deny his sensitivity to her, but he knew. He knew what she'd been afraid of, though she'd been too afraid to acknowledge it even to herself. He'd sensed the half-buried fear that she felt whenever she wondered if she was losing that ever-present sense of other people, the constant, tiring, familiar invasion of another's emotions and sometimes thoughts. She'd managed to keep her fear at bay by succeeding in reaching out to her mother's awareness and capturing, by conscious effort, that sensitivity to thought and emotion. But the fear had been there and he had known.

She pushed herself off the bed and retreated as far away as possible from the now still and silent man who had invaded her thoughts and awareness, and now her privacy. Then she turned to face him, like an animal at bay. She said bitterly, her voice quivering, 'At least in my entire life, I have never been cruel to another person with the knowledge my sensitivity brings me. Look at what you'd said. And tell me, looking back, just why you said it!' She waited a moment and listened to his silence. Finally she whispered, 'See? You're lying to yourself more than you really know. Now, get out. I've had enough for one night. I don't want to listen to you anymore.'

With that she leaned against the side of her window

and stared out at the grey dawn. Tears eased out and crept sneakily down her cheeks. She heard him move, sensed his intention, and she shrank against the wood as if she were trying to ooze through it to reach the outdoors. But the wood and the room, and the man trapped her and she did nothing but quiver as his hand came down gently to her shoulders and turned her around. He very gently put his arms around her and held her close to his warm, bare chest.

After a long silence, he said softly, 'The only thing I've ever done to you is hurt you, one way or another. I'm sorry. The last thing I'd ever want to do to you is hurt you. I'm sorry.'

'It's not true,' she whispered, leaning her head on his shoulder and letting him take her weight as her eyelids fell shut. 'But when are you going to stop hurting yourself?'

After a time, David eased his head back to look down at her tired, sleeping face. Then, with an infinite gentleness, he carefully picked her up and eased her on to the bed, drawing the covers up over her. She opened her eyes once and looked at him with a grave, owlish look that, combined with the slenderness of her neck and the pallor of her face, made her look like a small, solemn child. It made him smile. Her lids fluttered closed again, this time for good, and her breathing deepened.

He stood over her for quite some time, stroking the hair that was splayed out over the white pillowcase, his eyes containing something dark, his own visage exhausted. Then he stirred, unaware that Denise and Peter had come to the open doorway and were watching him silently, worriedly. With that great weariness that had seeped into every one of his bones, that had built up over the years, he whispered the answer to her as if she'd just uttered the question.

'I don't know when, Dana. I just don't know when.'

The two silent people at the doorway glided away without a sound. Then, after a time, David stirred himself again and left.

CHAPTER EIGHT

DANA slept well into the next day and when she woke up, it was with a feeling of refreshment. After a quick and horrified glance at her clock, she edged out of her bed and slipped on her bathrobe, intent on heading for the shower. As she walked out of her bedroom and into the hall, she heard voices floating up the staircase, and she stopped stock still as a feeling of amazement and dismay flooded through her. Why hadn't she known?

No one could have surprised Dana in the past. It didn't matter if she was particularly sensitive to a person or not, she always knew when someone other than family was in the house, just as she always knew when they were about to receive a long distance phone call, though she occasionally didn't know who was calling. She groped out mentally, her dismay making her clumsy, putting quite a lot of effort into it. Before anything had had a chance to register, she heard David's deep voice roaring from the living room, impatience and pain tingeing his bellow.

'Dana, for the love of Heaven, will you cut that out?'

She jumped violently, completely disconcerted, and footsteps came rapidly down the hall. David's large bulk appeared at the bottom of the stairs and he paused, one foot resting on the first step, his expression now concerned. 'What is it? What's frightened you?' he called up.

She pulled herself up tight, clamped down on the turbulence in her, and said irritably, 'Nothing. Nothing at all! Excuse me.' With that she whirled and dashed into the bathroom, and shut and locked the door. She showered furiously, rubbing at her tender skin until it was red, and roughly shampooing her hair in deliberate ignorance of her smarting scalp. Then she marched back to her room, slammed the door and dressed as jerkily and as haphazardly as she'd showered, yanking at a delicate summer top so hard that a spaghetti string snapped. She threw it viciously into a corner and yanked on another. Dragging a comb through her thick, long hair, she then tossed it back over her shoulder where it fell with a damp plop, and she marched out of her room and down the stairs.

When she went into the kitchen, she found it occupied, with her mother at the coffee maker and both Peter and David sitting at the table. Everyone looked up when she entered. She nodded shortly to Peter, looked once at David, and touched her mother on the shoulder as she went by. She opened the refrigerator, hearing absolutely nothing behind her. She clamped down on her thoughts and feelings instinctively, trying to shut out the possibility of David inquiring into her mind. She then heard behind her a muffled sound like a snort of laughter, but she wouldn't allow herself the luxury of turning around to see who it was.

She grabbed out the milk and slammed the cubicle's door shut, whisked a box of cereal down from the cupboard, and slammed them on the table before going back for a spoon. The only available chair was next to David.

As she opened the box and started to shake out some corn flakes, the man beside her moved and put both hands down flat on the table as he asked flatly, 'Okay, what gives?'

Dana looked up and encountered three pairs of interested eyes on her, one pair full of impatience and too close for comfort. 'There's no privacy in this world, is there?' she muttered, hunching a shoulder. She splashed milk into the bowl and then dumped a spoonful of sugar on top of everything, glaring at it furiously as if she wanted to pick it up and throw it across the room for just sitting there.

'Both your mother and Peter know fully well what is going on between us,' he said very softly, as she jabbed her spoon into her soggy cereal. He leaned forward as if to stare her down. 'They aren't going to be shocked or surprised by anything said.'

'And who's fault is that?' she snapped irritably, her eyes, mouth and neck taut with effort to suppress her frustration and upset. It wasn't working.

'Why, you little——' he bit out.

'Don't swear at me, I won't——' she exploded, standing furiously.

He surged to his feet also. '—And you're dictating my behaviour, now, is that——'

'—Because you're striking out with absolutely no——'

'—I've had a hell of a lot of provocation, and it's not exactly——'

'Shut up! Shut up!' Dana clapped her hands over her ears as she screamed, and the metal spoon she still held smacked painfully and wetly against her ear.

'Ouch!' David thundered, seeming bigger than life

because of his anger. He clapped a right hand to his ear. 'Dammit, you nearly took off——'

Taking both fists, she pounded once on the table, very hard, and she yelled furiously, '—And it's *my* blessed ear, not yours, so get out of my head, will you?' And all four of them watched as the full bowl of cereal and milk that she'd knocked with the spoon still clenched in her hand, arced up into the air, almost in slow motion, to flip twice and spew its content of soggy flakes all over the table, the wall, and both Dana and David. The bowl clattered to the floor with an ear splitting *crack!* and the fragments shot out to speckle the tiled floor with jagged stoneware.

Dana looked at the floor in appalled silence after the accident, her face tight, her jaw jutting out and her expression fed up. Then without a backward glance, she marched for the door determinedly. On the way out she grabbed at the tea towel hanging on the refrigerator door latch and mopped her face. She stalked into the living room and threw herself on to the couch.

Peter said humorously, 'I suppose you two had a complete and intelligible argument underneath all that?' David shot him a piercing black glance, but it apparently bounced right off the older man's thick skin.

Denise said helplessly, 'I'm very sorry for Dana's behaviour today. I just don't know what to say.'

Peter stood up. 'Don't be sorry. Both David and Dana are responsible for their own actions, not you. They're both under a lot of stress, and it is, after all, understandable. And I think I might know what to say.' He too headed for the door, crunching on broken china, which Denise hastened to begin picking up.

David shot out a hand to halt Peter's progress. 'I think this time I'd better go and talk to her,' he said shortly.

Peter carefully removed the other man's hand. 'But I have a previous appointment,' he replied smilingly. 'Calm down a bit, David. There's plenty of time.'

David's lips tightened but he remained behind and let the slighter man have his way. After Peter left the room, he sighed, shook his head, and started to help clean up the mess left behind.

Dana didn't look up immediately when she heard someone enter the room. She'd instantly put all of her concentration on clamming up her fury and frustration, appalled at how she'd erupted like a volcano and determined not to let it happen again, no matter what David said. Then Peter was talking and she sagged with relief. She'd been expecting David.

'You do realise that it's all right to get upset and scream things out once in a while, don't you?' he asked her, smiling at her tense, unhappy face. The kindliness in his voice made her sniff madly. The older man's voice was gentle as he sat down next to her. 'Are you one of those people who are afraid to get angry and cause a scene?'

She nodded miserably, a sneaky tear slipping down her face. She swiped at it, angry at herself, and muttered, 'I've never shouted like that in my life. I . . . I don't know what came over me, I . . . he was so angry and tense, it . . . it beat at my head like a hammer and I couldn't get it out.'

And somehow she was telling him everything. It just poured out of her in a flood. Peter weathered the storm well, asking a quiet question here, interposing a word of encouragement there. She found herself telling of her horror and fear of the nightmares, how she'd thought she was going mad. She told him of the unbearable stretched tight feeling of the recent past, the strange waking nightmare of the day before, and her own attempted suicide. She told him of her recent lack of sensitivity, how she felt the world was being turned upside down on her, how she didn't know what to trust in herself any more. When she mentioned to him that she thought of herself as an aberration of normality, he interrupted.

'And do you really think you are so unique?' he queried quietly, smiling at her in such a way that she couldn't take offence at his words.

'I really don't know what to think,' she said wretchedly. 'I've nothing and no one to compare myself with.'

'And that is such an important part of our reality, isn't it? It gives us a measuring stick and a common bond with each other. In our own individualities, we are similar and yet separate entities. What is your reality, Dana?'

She brooded, chin tucked in and arms wrapped around herself. 'The awareness of my self and my awareness of others,' she finally whispered.

'And you are afraid that you are losing part of your reality.'

Echoing his words, she said, 'And I am afraid I am losing part of my reality.' And she couldn't keep her next words in: 'But my reality is so abnormal, it's not . . . I can't survive with it, and I can't survive without it!'

She covered her face and drew in a shuddering

breath. She didn't see the dark man appear soundlessly at the doorway, his questioning glance directed at Peter, who shook his head. David disappeared.

'Dana, listen to me a moment. Just listen to what you said. Do you know anything about psychic phenomena? Have you done any reading on the subject at all?' She felt one of her hands taken and forced down as Peter continued in his gentle, inexorable voice. 'I've been doing a little bit of reading on the subject since I've been told about you. It hasn't made me an expert on the subject, by any means, but it has been an eye opener in a lot of ways. Why should you view yourself as being abnormal? Why has this particular idea held on in your mind? We all—most of us, anyway—are presently using a mere fraction of our own brains. Who is to say either way whether your individual use of your mind is right or wrong? I certainly could not make such a judgment, and I've made medicine and the mind my life's work. And you must know that you're not the only one who has experienced some sort of Extra Sensory Perception. How can you explain away the psychic who helps police in their investigations of murder victims? How does one explain away the rocking chair that starts to move of its own volition in the middle of the day? How can one explain away a certain sense of danger or disaster that some people experience, or those who know just exactly when a loved one has died? The brain emits powerful waves of energy, Dana! What if these waves are somehow bouncing back and forth in a house, let off by the original mind of the occupant who has recently died? Do we call these old, unoriginal waves a ghost or poltergeist, fearing its existence?

There are hundreds of tales of people who have sensed what a loved one was thinking, though they are across a crowded room. How many times is this sheer intimate knowledge, or perhaps a crude telepathy? What is normality? Isn't your normality the existence of your particular gift?'

'I guess so,' she mumbled, almost afraid to trust the incredible easing of tension at his support.

'Don't carry your talent around as if it were a blemish on your soul. You are what you are, and though I'm a great believer of a person's ability to change for the better, there are some things one cannot alter. I will always be five foot eight. I may stoop more as I age, but I can never be four feet, nor seven feet tall. By the same token, dear girl, you have a powerful mind. It may at times be very hard to bear, but it is as precious as your very identity.' His hand tightened on her briefly and then dropped away.

'But I've never experienced anything as intensely as I have in the last few weeks with David,' she replied uncertainly, still groping for answers. 'And I've never felt this—this lessening of sensitivity. What if I am really losing it?'

'What's your mother doing?' Peter asked her, in such a normal, off hand manner that she answered quite without thinking.

'She's taking a roast out of the freezer—oh!' She laughed a bit shakily as she encountered his thoughtful gaze.

'At an educated guess, I'd say your talent is inherent in you, Dana, and though it may change as you change, you'll always have something in you of its nature.'

'Did—did David talk to you much about what—happened the day before yesterday?' she asked slowly and painfully.

Peter replied calmly, 'Yes, he did. And from what you've told me, if sounds like you all had quite a fright.'

'I've never been so terrified of myself in my life,' she whispered, pressing her fingers to her temples, where a headache was beginning to pound. 'I'd always been afraid that I would pick up a crazy person's rantings and go completely mad myself, and then I blanked out like I did, doing just as I'd feared, and——'

And she looked up with a gasp, because David was standing there, his face a total, unfamiliar mask. He gripped a glass of water until his knuckles were white and she thought the glass would shatter, and then he thrust it into her hand, along with a bottle of aspirin. 'Here,' he said emotionlessly, thrusting them both at her, as if he would like to throw them. 'They're for your headache.' And he disappeared before she had a chance to say anything.

Tears pricked at her eyes, and her face slowly crumpled into misery. Alarmed, Peter took a hold of the water glass, which had begun to shake violently. 'What's wrong, Dana?'

She looked at him sadly. 'He overheard what I said, she said dully. 'He thought that I'd meant him.

The sun was very bright, reminding her of the day when she'd nearly ended her life, the day of blackness. She trudged slowly up the hill, feeling the pleasurable tug of leg muscles, feeling them work. Now, instead of being dead, she was so very glad to be alive. As she reached the clearing on the hilltop, her eyes shot over to the pine tree and found him sitting there in the shade, gazing over the view, his face and mind closed against her scrutiny, completely walled off.

She walked over to sit down beside him, not too close, as she felt the pangs of uncertainty assail her. He never turned his head to acknowledge her presence, never so much as flickered an eyelid. She sighed. His head rested against the tree behind him, his dark hair falling back and brushing the wood, his profile rocklike, as hard as the bottom of the cliff. She searched his face, the expressionless eyes, the straight, thinned mouth, his hands on his knees. They clenched.

She flexed her fingers and spoke, softly, 'You misunderstood what you heard.'

No answer. Wind sighing, trees bowing, mind silence. She was at a loss, she didn't know how to break through this barrier, she didn't know what to say to him. He'd blocked himself up so, she wasn't even sure if she knew just exactly what was wrong. All she could do was guess. And the only thing she could do about it was to send to him a wordless wave of longing and intensity, and strong reassurance. She put everything she had into it. He flinched physically, bowed his head, ran his fingers through his dark, thick hair. His wide shoulders hunched.

'Get out of my head,' he muttered lowly, and it was such a shock to hear the words, so familiar from her, coming from someone else. Her mouth shook.

'Excuse me,' she whispered. 'I'm very sorry.' Feeling incredibly hurt, she stumbled to her feet and turned away, intent on getting far away from him, appalled that she had intruded on something she'd always valued more highly than anything else: a person's privacy.

She only made a few steps, only managed to get just beyond the shade of the pine trees and into the hot sunlight when something behind her moved, rustled, and then she was grabbed from behind, turned very roughly, and yanked into his arms, so hard the breath was knocked out of her. Surprise hit her hard, and she parted her lips on a shocked gasp. His mouth was swooping down on hers, lips shaking, teeth hard and bruising. She moaned, and then she was let go, only to have her shoulders gripped and shaken hard.

'Do you know what you're doing to me?' he shouted, dark eyes glittering. She stared into them, mesmerised. 'Do you know what you're doing to me?'

'Stop it!' she screamed, her hands on his wrists, twisting in an effort to get his grip loosened. 'Stop it! Stop it!'

And much to her horror and dismay, she watched as David stood stock still, his eyes widened and suddenly very vulnerable as the realisation of what he was doing to her sank in, and he slowly sank on to his knees in front of her, wrapped his arms quite gently around her waist, and buried his head in her stomach. Absolutely no sound came from him, but a shudder hit his frame, and then another, and she became even more horrified as she realised that he was crying.

Dana had never seen or heard a man cry before, and it was a terrible experience. The only man she'd ever been close to had been her father, and her memories of him were of a strong, self-reliant man; they were god-

like in their childish simplicity, and one-sided. All of
her impressions of David had been that he had been a
very powerful man, powerful in character, emotions
and instincts, and powerful in convictions. This sight
of him so vulnerable and in such need shook her to the
core. She couldn't take the sight.

'Oh, David. Oh, David,' she said, in words that
shook. Her hands went out, touched his hair, stroked
it tentatively. There was still no sound from him, and
the violent tremors had not ceased. She dug her
fingers into his hair and pulled his head back, her own
face crumbling. They stared at each other for a very
long time. She touched his wet face. His eyes were
bleeding. Her own shoulders quaked as she sank to her
knees and wrapped her arms around him as tightly as
she could.

Ribs aching from pressure, heart aching from pain,
she leaned her face into his neck and he rocked her
back and forth. His hard shoulders dug into the fleshy
part of her upper arm as she closed them about his
neck, his hard cheekbone jutting into her own soft
cheek, the wetness making it slippery. She wasn't sure
if the wetness was from him alone anymore, or if it
was from her. She wasn't sure of anything except the
bright yellow sunshine, her own chest ache, and his.

'What do I need from you?' he whispered. 'What do
I need? Why can't I get you out of my mind and my
life?'

At that she cried out, more hurt than she could
possibly say. She tried to get her arms away from him
and draw into herself, but he wouldn't let her. He took
her face between his big hands and searched her eyes.
His own were so close, she shut her eyes against it.

'What have I done to you?' he asked lowly. 'What have I done to myself? Why couldn't I let all of it go like others have, and carry on with my life, instead of becoming this strange sort of psychological cripple that can't even function——'

'And do you think you are so unique?' she returned very quietly, intentionally repeating Peter's words to her of not three hours before. 'Do you really think you have a corner on the market here? Oh, David, have you been talking to Peter at all?'

His features hardened, the bone jutting into the muscle, the face angling out. 'Some.'

'Then you know that Peter thinks we've experienced what he called a flashback experience. According to him, it happens to other Vietnam veterans. There were so many men thrust into a bizarre situation and a nightmarish way of life! In a matter of days, all of you were, after training, pushed into guerrilla warfare in a strange, surrealistic setting. Boys were expected to kill as a livelihood, and then after their eighteen months or two years, or whatever they were supposed to be serving, they were sent back home in a matter of days, no deprogramming, no deconditioning—*wham!* From fighting for your life in a jungle and watching your buddies die to suddenly peaceful Small Town, U.S.A. That's a severe culture shock to the system, David——'

'I should have been able to handle it!' he grated out, teeth white and snarling, his hands crunching her delicate bone structure. She winced. 'I was older! I saved lives, dammit, I didn't take them! I should have been able to handle it!'

His fury ignited hers. 'And, oh, save us from mister

God Almighty Himself!' she burst out angrily, jerking
her head out of his hold and pushing away from him
with both hands. She fell back into the dust, rolled
away, came to her knees and glared at him in fury.
'Why can't the simple fact sink into your skull that
you are just a man! Just one man, David! Stop tying
all of those destructive feelings up in a bundle and let
them out before you fester until you'll never be well!
Look at whom you're talking to!' She pounded at her
own chest, hurting herself in her anger. 'I know what
happened, too! I know about those dreams and the
horror! I experienced the flashback!'

'And I have to live with that fact!' he roared,
pounding the ground with a huge, clenched fist. He
frightened her so much, she jumped, eyes huge on
him. His shoulders were hunched, one hand supporting his weight while he glared at her as if he hated her.

'Do you think I don't?' she whispered. 'I've never
held a gun in my life. I've never lost control like that
before in my life. I've never tried to commit suicide,
and I have to live with that!'

'Because of me,' he said tightly.

'No, David. Because of me.' Her eyes were sick. He
sucked in a deep breath. 'It's me. You probably would
have been able to have your nice little crisis, all by
yourself, all alone like you'd planned. Do you think I
don't know? That's why you took a break away from
work, isn't it, because you felt the pressure and the
rage and the memory building? Only I stupidly
interfered, didn't I? I wasn't something you'd
expected. And the dreams that plagued you *I* had, and
I couldn't handle them. You were the strong one; if it
hadn't been for you and your self-containment, I

would have broken under the pressure long ago. I was the weak one——'

'You shouldn't have had to handle it,' he said achingly.

She looked at him and echoed, 'You shouldn't have had to handle all of that, either.'

'Don't say that.'

'It's the truth! Remember that dream when you said that you didn't believe in hell? You still keep denying it, and it's what has festered over the years! David, there is a hell. No matter how you must have wanted to, you couldn't save the world from it, then.'

She closed her fist over her heart, as if taking a hold of something. It was wholly unconscious. His eyes were closed, his throat worked. 'You can't cut that out of you. Vietnam is a part of you, and it's a part of me now. I don't know, it may be a part of everyone. It may be in the past, but it's there, and you may try to block it all you like. It's there.'

'It doesn't have to be a part of you!' he grated, shaking his head like a stubborn bull. 'I can stop that at least. It won't be a part of you, too! Not you.' He looked up, the piercing of his glance lancing her through. She ached so. 'Peter told you, I'm sure, that he thought we were entwined in this—this crisis together because we'd needed what the other had. God only knows what you needed from me. I don't.' Don't you? she asked silently. Don't you yet? 'But I must have needed your weakness. I must have needed someone else to show me that. I'm sorry it had to be you that helped me to exorcise my ghosts. At least it's over now.'

'I'm not!' she cried. 'It isn't.' He stood, and the

finality of his stance, along with the long look he gave her, filled her with the oddest kind of fear. 'David?' No, wait! Don't walk away!' This, before he'd even made a move.

He smiled. 'I can't do anything around you without you knowing of it, can I? But I must, sweet Dana. I have to, for the both of us, and especially for you. You don't really think that I couldn't feel your lie, when you said to me that it wouldn't matter if I went away, do you? It took me a while to understand what I was sensing, but I have. You don't really think that I don't know?'

She felt as if she'd been kicked. 'David? If you know that, then you know that I——'

'Don't say it! Please don't say it,' he said harshly. 'This can't happen, not to you, not to me. This can't be allowed.'

He's doing it again, she thought dazedly. He's blocking himself off, only this time he's blocking himself off from me. She put both hands over her shaking mouth, eyes filled with tears, watching the blur of him that seemed suddenly miles and miles away.

'Don't look at me that way, girl!' he roared at her furiously. 'Do you realise what we'd do to each other, what I'd do to you? For the love of Heaven, get out of my life before it's too late!'

She stumbled to her feet. Get out of his life, you heard him, Dana. She turned like an automaton. He knew. He knew all the time. And he was right there, pulling her into his arms, surrounding her, kissing her like a madman, thrusting his tongue into her mouth ferociously, trying to eat every bit of her in that last embrace. Then he thrust her from him, whispering, 'Get out of my life, Dana.'

Some time later she managed to walk into the kitchen with some degree of calm. Her mother, who was reading a magazine, looked up with an encouraging smile. 'Oh, good, it's you. I started to get a bit worried,' said Denise. Her expression changed as she took in the utterly blank façade on her daughter's face. 'What's happened now?'

Dana just looked at her. 'I gave my love,' she replied flatly, 'and had it thrown back in my face.'

CHAPTER NINE

IN the next few days, Dana's schedule managed to right itself well enough. The tense feeling of imminent disaster eased, as did the nightmares, and she began to relax, feeling that the crisis was well and truly over with. She talked to Peter once on the phone, and she told him that her days seemed to be slipping into a certain peacefulness which was soul healing and revitalising. Her mind was at ease like never before, for the one thing that she honestly felt that David had been able to somehow convey to her was his mental ability to block. It gave her a measure of control that she'd never had; it soothed her mind like nothing she'd ever known. She listened to the mental silence, revelled in it, and blossomed. She had achieved an apparently surpassable barrier, and could reach out with her mind. If she was sensitive to a person, like her mother, then she could feel their presence. It gave her a retreat, an important feeling of detachment.

On the second day after her climactic confrontation with David, she went to see Grace Cessler, for the first time without a mental flinch at the visit. She indeed had a nice time; she'd inched out once with her mind and assured herself of the older woman's easing of pain, for she was sure that Grace would not hesitate to lie about it. They both had a pleasant hour, with only one uncomfortable spot when Grace mentioned that David was planning on moving at the end of the month. The news jolted Dana. She hadn't any warning of his coming departure, and this told her that he must be working hard at blocking her totally. The feeling of rejection hurt like an open wound.

On the way back from seeing Grace, Dana stopped at the grocery store, more confident than ever about stepping out into a public place. She came upon a young married woman in one of the aisles, who had over the last several months made overtures of friendliness to her. Dana responded to the sight of Jenny with pleasure, and soon the two were talking comfortably away while Dana held Jenny's young daughter on her hip and laughed to see the child's contortions as she chomped on a teething ring.

Jenny, who lived down the street from Dana, mentioned to her brightly, 'Did you know that the local Garden Club is sponsoring a great monster of a party down in the gymnasium across from the court house?'

Dana shook her head, smilingly. 'Why are they doing that?' she asked. 'Is there a chance to make money out of it?'

Jenny sent her a look that was droll. 'Of course. They're selling tickets, which by the way, happen to be pretty reasonable. I have a few with me, if your mother and you would care to go. There've been other parties in the past, but I've always been afraid to invite you two, because you seemed so shy. Silly, isn't it? I'm glad I've found you really aren't hard to talk to. Isn't it strange, the ideas we form of people without really knowing them?'

Dana's smile turned wry. If Jenny only knew. 'How

much are the tickets?' she asked, digging into her jeans pocket. 'Why don't you give me two of them?'

'They're only four dollars apiece, which will get you in and get you supper. There will be alcoholic drinks, and of course other types of drinks, but you have to pay for those.' They exchanged tickets for money, and Jenny beamed at Dana happily. 'Two more tickets sold! My mother makes me so mad! She volunteers to sell more tickets than she can, and gives half to me, and I don't even belong to the Club! Oh, Dana, I'm glad you're going! You need some night life, although this isn't quite the definitive of the word! It still should be fun, though. See you Saturday!'

Dana had to grin at herself and the eagerness that she felt at the prospect of going to the party on Saturday. Previously, the old Dana would have cringed in horror at the very thought of being with so many people in one place, but now, with her new found assurance, she felt excited and happy at the thought, feeling for the first time in her life burden-free of her fears.

Grabbing her notebook when she got home, she lightly kissed her mother on the cheek and headed out of doors to do some sketching. Instead of taking a familiar route, she delved into the wood and ended up on the far side of Grace's property, in a little pocket of land she'd never really explored before. The land dipped into a hollow, at the bottom of the cliff, and then some distance away rose to the peak of a very gentle hill. She was able to position herself on the top of the hill at the break of some trees and obtain a perfect view of the rocky cliff, with the green, perpetually swaying pines above it and the jutting line of the edged rock below. It was a perspective she'd never seen before, and beautiful. She drew out her pencil to capture it on paper.

After a time of solitude and silence, she looked up and to her left. Just coming into view from a thick line of trees was a dark, slow moving figure of a man. Her pencil plopped to the ground and she stood clumsily. Her movement attracted his attention, and his head reared up at the sight of her. He jerked to a halt.

Suddenly the feelings that she'd kept at bay for the last few days threatened to make her sight blur, and she mumbled, 'Excuse me. I'll leave now.' Almost at random, she reached and found her pad and pencil, and with her head ducked, she started to scurry away, intent on leaving before he could reject her again.

'Dana?' he called out lowly, the sound urgent. She quivered to a halt, shoulders held stiff. She didn't dare turn around to look at him. Even the sight of David was enough to break through her barriers. No matter how she may try, she knew that he was the one she couldn't keep out of her mind and her heart. 'Dana, please, look at me.'

'No. What do you want?' Heart ache. Her pencil snapped in her hand and brought back a strange feeling of *déjà vu*.

'Don't go. I'm sorry for disturbing you. I—really hadn't realised, at least consciously that you were here. I'll leave.' His voice was gentle, but it wasn't his gentleness she wanted. She didn't want his empathy either. She just wanted his love.

There was nothing but silence behind her and she turned around, eyes full of longing and hand involuntarily stretched out—and he was still there, just watching her, very still. She'd expected him gone, and the barriers she'd let drop were totally swept away as she was filled with the essence of his intensity, his own turbulent emotions. She hissed as she sucked in her breath and jerked her hand to her side, and suddenly he was rushing for her, pulling at her, dragging her down to the ground and covering her with his superior weight. Then his hands were fastening in her hair and yanking her head around as his hungry mouth searched her face for her lips.

She could have been frightened. She very well could have been alarmed, having never experienced the overwhelming physical aspect of a relationship. Whether it was herself or him that she was attuned to, she later couldn't say. All she knew was her own instinctive desire to mate, and her own physical need she had to fill, and her own hands found their way to the back of David's head. She eagerly arched her back against the hard ground, pressing her body to his, a timeless invitation.

After a flash of eternity, she felt him drag back his hands from under her top and roll away, breathing unsteadily. She took a deep, unsteady breath herself and stared up at the swaying green oak branches overhead, with blue sky peeping through. Her chest and ribs were damp from the heat of the day and her own passion, and she raised a limp hand to wipe her sticky hair off her forehead. The fingers shook.

'I'm sorry,' he muttered, still sucking in his breath and striving for control. 'It won't hap——'

'But of course you're sorry,' Dana said calmly, and Dana being calm after the powerful storm of sexuality that had just shuddered through her was enough to make him stare, head lifted, strong muscles in his neck taut. She turned her head as she lay there and just looked at him, face almost amused. 'That's all you've ever been, isn't it? All your adult life you've been sorry that you didn't save the kid who died, sorry that you weren't the great hero that saved the world, sorry that you couldn't control the emotion that was uncontrollable. I wonder if every man is like this, always on a god trip and never able to take time to be human and fallible. Of course you're sorry, you've never let yourself be anything but.'

'Don't lecture me, Dana,' he grated, eyes turning hard. 'God, look at you, you're so young and inexperienced, how the hell can you expect to know what I'm all about?'

'Oh, to be sure,' she said sardonically, very quietly. 'I don't know anything. Especially me, of all people. I wouldn't know what it felt like to have a knife slide into my gut, I wouldn't know the utter hell of futility and my own incapacity to save five bleeding kids from death. I don't know what it's like to——'

'*No, you don't!*' he roared, surging up and above her. She cowered away instinctively, but he wouldn't let her slip away as he planted his two hands on either side of her, pinning her to the ground. 'You didn't have to live with that for thirteen years!'

'Neither did you,' she came back, implacable.

'What the hell do you want from me?' he jerked out angrily. She'd never seen a man so cornered and so free to move away.

'That's just it, I don't want anything from you,' she replied earnestly. 'No, really, I don't. I've learned a great deal from you and from some things you've taught me, I'll be eternally grateful. You didn't know that I'd managed to pick up something of your ability to block things, did you? It's been wonderful, the most peace I've enjoyed in my life, and for that I thank you.' She pushed at one of his arms and he fell back to stare at her while she sat up, leaves in her chestnut hair still tumbled from his rough and urgent hands. She looked at him with clear eyes and gestured behind her. 'But what almost happened here wasn't right, because you'd have felt a burden of guilt for it and probably would have conveyed it to me, and making wonderful love is something I don't want to feel guilty about. Do you understand me? I don't want your guilt. That's why I'm not going to ask for one thing from you, I won't have that guilt on me. You're not prepared to give anything freely. No, I'm going to sit back and do nothing, and let the burden of decision fall on you. You seem to like burdens well enough. You see, I may not be very strong for some of the things that you've had to endure, but this is one thing I'm strong enough for. I'm not going to back out and walk away. I'm willing to stay and take the risk of whatever might happen. You can stay or leave, it's up to you. It's always been up to you.'

He turned away, and she felt her heart sink, even though she'd not expected anything else. But at his next words, she felt a wild beat of hope begin to surge in her chest. 'I need to think,' he said heavily. 'I need to think.' But then he looked at her, and the angry, mixed up emotion in his eyes and his last words before he walked away made her heart sink again. 'Don't expect too much from me, Dana. I won't take emotional manipulation.'

'When will you realise that you are as free as you will let yourself be?' she whispered. 'I don't expect anything from you. Just live and be happy, not haunted.'

He walked away, and in the silence of his leaving, she wondered why it still could hurt to see him walk away when with her he had never done anything else.

Dana nervously halted on the outside of the closed door, from which party sounds were emitting. She smoothed down the skirt of her light green dress and looked to her mother for reassurance. 'Oh, Mom, does my dress look all right? Did I smudge my make up in the car? Maybe I should go and check in the rearview mirror——'

Denise smiled at her daughter fondly and grasped her arm with a very firm grip. 'No, you shouldn't check yourself in the mirror! You checked yourself not three minutes before, and you look marvellous! Come on, Dana, where's your sense of adventure and spirit?'

'I knew I forgot something,' Dana grumbled goodnaturedly, ruefully grinning.

'The people in that building are only a number of single individuals, and you have always managed things well with one person at a time. It's not like you don't know anybody! Come on now, and quit stalling!'

And so Dana reluctantly followed her mother into the huge gymnasium that the Garden Club had rented and decorated, her mind tightly closed against any unwelcome intrusion. It was perhaps a good thing she'd blocked herself so well, for the physical shock of so many people together and chatting and laughing all at once jolted her senses as it was. She felt overwhelmed at the noise level, the people, the heat, the press, for she had never really experienced or been capable of experiencing a crowd of any size.

Her mother was right ahead of her, and Dana saw her turn to give her a sharp glance. 'Are you all right so far? This isn't too much for you, is it?' she asked lowly.

Dana smiled, an uncertain movement and yet genuinely amused. 'I can't tell yet. The noise level is too loud for me to think! No, I think I'll do just fine. I just have to get used to so many people in one place.' Her eyes scanned the large open area, and she had to laugh again. 'It's funny, isn't it? My mind intellectually tells me that there can't be more than two hundred people here, and yet my brain is reeling.'

'You aren't used to a crowd. Take it easy and stick by me until you feel you are able to take it on your own. Remember, we can always leave.'

Dana's eyes, large from her new experience, had begun to sparkle. She looked over the people, all so differently and brightly attired in light summer clothes, all chatting and laughing and mixing together. 'I rather think,' she murmured, 'that I'm going to enjoy myself tonight, after all. Did you ever see so many people?' And she grinned as her mother laughed. 'Look! There's Jenny. Let's go and say hello.'

Denise was agreeable, and so they threaded their way through the people to Jenny's side, and the slim young woman turned to give them both a wide, welcoming smile. 'Hello!' she called out merrily, looking pleased. 'I'm glad you could come—my mother and I were wondering if you'd really show or not. We've been keeping an eye peeled on the door, but you must've sneaked in on us.' Jenny's mother, Mrs Bernstein, turned around at her daughter's words and soon Dana was feeling as if she'd been literally swept under a large mother hen's wing. It was a rather flustering feeling, but very nice and welcoming, and soon her mother was chatting away with Mrs Bernstein. Jenny motioned with her eyes to Dana.

'Come on,' she whispered. 'When my ma starts, no power on this earth can stop her, and I don't really care to hear all about planting tomatoes right now, if you know what I mean. Let's go and get supper.' Dana smilingly followed Jenny to a buffet table that was laden with food and they each heaped their plates, talking the whole while. Dana met several people that she knew; she'd never realised how many people she really did have an acquaintance with. There was the grocer and his family, and the postman and the bookstore clerk. All expressed pleasure at seeing Dana, and she felt a wave of warmth from their smiles.

Finally Jenny and she turned to make their way to a seat and Dana had to stop suddenly to avoid the male body that blocked her way. As her eyes travelled up the dark length of David's muscular body, she felt a thrill of shock, almost as if she were meeting him for the first time. He was wearing a dark smart pair of slacks and a white shirt, rolled up to the elbows, and it wasn't so much his attire but the way he held himself that made her heart jolt. He was looking right down into her eyes, expression withdrawn, eyes searching, and then he slowly smiled, starting with his eyes and then widening his lips. It was a genuine, open smile, and he looked younger and more attractive than she'd realised was possible. She knew that most people wouldn't call him handsome in the strict sense of the word, but to her he was the most beautiful person in the world. And he was smiling at her.

Jenny was speaking, '. . . and I would like for you to meet our neighbour, David Raymond, or have you two already met?' Her bright eyes watched them avidly.

'I know him,' Dana said quietly, and the very quality of her voice made the words somehow more than a simple statement. She smiled again but then turned away. 'Excuse us, David. You're welcome to join us, if you'd like, but——' a flash from over her shoulder, '—don't feel obligated.'

Jenny made some laughing remark and Dana heard David's low voice in reply. Then Dana was sitting down at a table, trying desperately to get herself together, wondering at how her heart was racing madly along, at her giddy happiness at seeing him so unexpectedly, at her foolish hope every time she looked into his eyes. Her mental block faltered just for a moment, and suddenly she looked up, across the room, her face paling. There, across people's heads, stood a lazy, insolent, lounging figure, his face obscured by some shadow, but she knew it was Mick. She'd know that wave of antipathy anywhere. She watched him, upset as he mockingly raised a beer bottle to her and then drank, a cold trickle of the liquid slithering down his cheek and neck. She swallowed and then turned away.

And she looked up at David, who stood frowningly in front of her. 'What is it?' he asked, abruptly, setting his laden plate down and sitting. 'What's upset you?'

Another swallow and a glance away. 'Nothing, you must have imagined it,' she said lowly. Her fingers crept to the napkin by her plate and twisted into it. A large hand captured her restless fingers.

'Dana,' a low quiver ran through his voice and, startled, her eyes flew up to encounter vivid laughter in his lit, dark eyes. 'Don't lie to me, of all people. Where have I heard that one before?'

Her lips quavered into a smile. 'Really, it's nothing. A—a bad feeling that's passed. I don't want to talk about it here, please.'

'All right.'

She asked impulsively, 'Do you ever sense anyone else now?'

'No,' he said slowly, looking at her. 'Only you.' Her eyes dropped in confusion.

Jenny's laughing voice spoke behind them, 'I guess you do know each other if you hold hands over a cold buffet! No, honestly, Dana, I didn't know that any of the younger girls blushed these days! I'm only kidding, for Heaven's sake! Here, I got you a glass of wine.'

'Oh, let me pay you for it,' Dana said, thanking her for the cold glass.

'Goodness, no. Buy me a glass later on, will you? Have you tried the seafood salad, yet? I hear it's very, very good . . .'

Dana thought she'd never enjoyed herself so much as she did eating supper with David and Jenny, laughing in helpless surprise at David's incredible dry wit and Jenny's quick, droll response. Everywhere there were laughing people, and yet the trio was in an island of their own enjoyment, and Dana's vivid sparkling eyes told of her inner joy.

When she got up to get herself some dessert, she found David at her elbow, his manner attentive. At this she became so flustered that he laughed and again asked her what was wrong, this time his voice teasing, as if he already knew, which he probably did.

But though he teased, Dana nearly became tearful she was so earnest. 'I know that you probably realise that this is a first for me,' she said, painfully honest, gesturing around her. 'But you don't have to feel obligated to—to stay with me, if that's why——'

'Dana,' he said softly, coming closer and running a finger across her mouth until her lips trembled. He watched them as if fascinated, and she felt her knees quake. 'I'm with you because I want to be with you. Is that what you wanted me to say?'

She drew back, hurt. 'I wanted you to tell me the truth,' she whispered stiffly.

Suddenly he opened up and let something out, something brief. 'I was telling the truth,' he said simply.

She regarded him sombrely for a moment and then smiled. 'Thank you.' And she threw back her head and laughed out loud as he mockingly bowed low in front of her, eyebrow cocked, mouth slanted.

And the night became a fairy tale for Dana, who laughed and danced and lived each moment as if it were something precious to be treasured but not grasped at, letting go of each moment gently, letting it slide into memory, content to go on to the next. She caught sight of David's dark eyes on her more than once, contemplative, serious, and at first she would falter into silence, but she gradually felt more at ease and started to grin at him, once wrinkling her nose until he laughed.

'How can you be so simply happy?' he asked her, as he extended his hand out in invitation to lead her out to the dance floor.

She became thoughtful as she felt the warmth and the hardness of his arms close around her carefully. She lifted her face to David's suddenly attentive, still expression and she said quietly, 'Perhaps it's because I've had no expectations. I never dared to before, you know. Life for me was merely survival. I—it teaches you something about living, I guess. It makes you appreciate what you have at the moment.'

There wasn't any smile in David's eyes at that; there wasn't any glimmer of amusement at all. In fact as she looked up into his eyes, she surprised a strangely widened, remembering look, and his arms tightened until she felt her ribs ache. They circled the floor slowly, and slowly Dana eased her head on to his shoulder. He brought his face down and nestled in her hair for a while, cradling her close.

As the evening wore on, Dana became aware of a minor disturbance over near the bar, and she saw Mick and another young man, their faces flushed, as they started to get obnoxious. She stared at them, her face perplexed as she tried to understand what made them tick. Almost instinctively, she reached out with her mind and she caught such a welter of jumbled emotions that she actually reeled from the impact. Cloudy aggression, recklessness, a frustrated, un-realised malice overtopping sheer, constant boredom and resentment made her gasp and hold her head, and David's arm shot around her as they walked back to the tables where Denise and Mrs Bernstein were sitting. 'Dana? Dana?' he was asking sharply, shaking her shoulder roughly in an effort to get her head cleared. 'Dana, answer me! What is it?'

She looked at him and tried to smile. 'Nothing. No, don't look at me like that, David! There's nothing you can do about it! It's just something who has to fight their own battles and work out their problems on their own. Please, it's so unpleasant, just let it be.' They had reached the table and as the two women had seen Dana's momentary dizziness, there were anxious questions to counter and concerned attention to bear, so he didn't press the matter, but his eyes followed her around thoughtfully.

The two young men at the bar were finally approached by a stern looking woman with a double chin, both of which were bouncing in indignation, and they were politely but firmly shown the door, to everyone's evident relief. 'In fact,' Jenny said caustically, 'I can't imagine why they showed up here in the first place, but they always do! Mick's mother is a member of the club and I guess she coerces him into making an appearance. He's never too happy about it and neither is anyone else, since the chances are of him ending up just like he did tonight—filthy drunk. Well, the price for a drink at one of these things is always pretty low, even with the cover charge, so it's not too surprising that he does come.'

Instead of feeling relief that the two had finally left, Dana felt a strange and uneasy apprehension. It wasn't anything substantiated, and certainly not understood, so she put it down to over-stimulation and tried to dismiss it from her mind.

The room had cooled off quite a bit as the evening wore on. Some twenty minutes later, as David politely left the table to get a refill for both Mrs Berenstein and Denise, Jenny stood also and grinned down at her mother. 'I left my cardigan in the car,' she stated cheerfully. 'Be back in a minute.' And she headed out with her mother's admonition to bring her wrap, too.

It was a very normal incident, nothing unusual in any way. Everything in fact was so normal-seeming and innocuous that when Dana got a sudden rush of uncomfortable warmth as she watched Jenny's figure make for the exit, she was quite unprepared for it and gasped for air. She needed some fresh air. Maybe that would cool her off. She pushed against the table and stumbled to her feet. A shocking feeling of dread descended on her. Something was wrong. Something was going to be very wrong. Jenny. Without bothering to say anything in explanation to the two startled parents sitting there and gaping at her odd behaviour, she whirled and set off for the door, walking swiftly. She was so hot, and something impelled her feet into faster steps, and her breath came in faster, shorter gasps, and by the time she was out of the building and looking for Jenny, she was quite agitated.

Afterwards, Dana could never say quite how or why, but she realised that her heightened emotion and tense concentration somehow clicked her into a higher awareness. She wasn't sure how it happened, for she'd never experienced anything like it before.

As her eyes adjusted to the darkness after the light and the noise from inside, she suddenly saw several things. A wave of antipathy hit her, along with unreasoning recklessness, and she saw Mick and his friend as they laughed drunkenly in his car. He reached forward and turned on the ignition, revving the engine far too much.

The sound came from her right. It was then that she realised with a jolt that she'd seen them with her mind and not her eyes. She turned, knowing where to look now, and the pieces of her own apprehension began to tilt into place with a frightful rapidity that galvanised her into action. Jenny had just made her way to the last car parked in the row by the street and was heading for the outside door, the driver's side. She turned her hand to the floodlight's glare, head bent, searching for the car key to unlock the door.

Mick was in the mood for excitement. The danger in him had built with the drink and the boredom, and now he was ready for some action, some kind of thrill. As he squealed out of the parking space down the street and to Jenny's right, he saw what he could do.

Dana had divined his thought even as he thought it, and a scream of warning ripped from her throat as she leaped into a dead run from a standing still position. Her awareness fragmented into a triple awareness. She heard and felt herself, and the pull of the muscles in her legs as they responded to her punishing order. She saw Jenny's head jerk up and turn her way, and then the other girl started to walk towards her worriedly. She saw David's head jerk up also, though he was inside, and then he was roaring and sprinting for the door on the toes of his feet, just too far away to help. She saw and felt Mick's assumption, a drunk's assumption, that he was in control of the car as he shot it down the road towards Jenny. Jenny had come away clear from the car by now. Mick would give her a scare and himself a thrill, and after all, it was no big deal. Dana saw the car's speed and knew he'd never stop it or swerve in time.

And she felt so gloriously alive, as the adrenalin pumped into her veins and heightened her awareness and speed. She felt every single breath that she sucked in, every pulse beat, every footfall on the pavement. She saw the harsh light and black darkness, and she saw David smash through the doors, making them slam against the walls, straining with everything inside of him to get to her. She saw Mick's laughing, vivid face with her mind, saw it change into an expression of total horror as awareness hit too late. And she felt, as she raced, the utter sureness of her success.

She cannoned into Jenny with every ounce of her pelting, straining body, and shoved the other girl as violently as she could with both arms. Jenny was propelled backwards. Mick swerved to avoid them both, but he was swerving much too late, and as he had to yank the car to the left to avoid the parked cars to his right, he was bound to plough right into Dana. The metal thumped as he separated Dana from Jenny. The car didn't stop even then, though Mick was frantically applying the brakes, and it careened into the second row of parked vehicles, scoring three badly before crunching to a stop.

And everything in the world was screaming: Dana was screaming as she knew the futility of attempting to throw herself out of the way. She'd put everything into her dash to push Jenny aside. And David was roaring with rage and terror as he watched the whole

scene, so near and yet so irrevocably far away, sick with the
knowledge that no matter how hard he was racing, he
would never, ever be able to undo what was
happening. And Jenny was screaming as the right
bumper of the car knocked her stunningly away, and
the car's metal was screaming, and Mick was
screaming, and it did no good as he hit Dana full on.
She felt the blow right in her midsection, and it
smashed the air totally out of her. She remembered
that, as she tumbled through the air like a rag doll,
hitting the ground with an appalling force and rolling
over several times until she finally came to a halt some
yards away from the scarred cars. Everything had
seemed so strange as the world flashed, first the night
air and then the ground and then the air and then the
ground, in such a fast progression she felt as if she
would never know what was down or up again.

She lay on her back, out of air and hurting inside so
badly that she knew something had to be broken,
somewhere. She couldn't even moan, as she desperately
tried and tried to suck in air, one arm flung helplessly
out, her legs curled, head lolling to one side. She looked
like a broken doll as she lay there, trying to gasp for
breath. There were cries. Someone was screaming, and
Dana knew it was Jenny. With a gigantic effort, she
turned her head an inch or so and saw Jenny pick herself
up from her fall. A solid bulk hurtled to her side. David
knelt beside her, holding out both hands as if he wanted
very badly to touch her but was afraid to, his face blank
with shock, harsh bitten. She stared up at him, eyes wide
and frightened, and something welled up in her throat to
trickle down the side of her mouth, running down her
cheek. She couldn't breathe, labouring painfully.

David turned around and screamed at the people starting to run their way, his voice deep with the panic inside of him, 'Someone call an ambulance! She's very badly hurt! Damn it to hell, *hurry!*' He whirled back to Dana and touched her face with a violently trembling hand. 'Oh, darling, oh, God.'

'Is she alive? Oh, please, is she?' Jenny was sobbing nearby. Dana wanted to turn her head to reassure her, but she couldn't move anything anymore. She felt like a heavy piece of lead, like she was never going to move again.

'Yes,' he said curtly, and he started to very carefully press at her arms in order to see if either one was broken. People were shouting, crying out, and Dana vaguely realised that her mother was kneeling on her other side and saying something as Mrs Bernstein supported her, but Dana had eyes only for David. She watched him reach up to his shoulder, a fast and impatient movement, and he ripped his shirt sleeve right off, taking the cloth and carefully wiping at the trickle of blood coming from her mouth. His fingers still trembled uncontrollably, and he knelt with his face down close to hers.

The adrenalin had stopped pumping. Something was wailing in the distance and getting louder, an inhuman sound, insistent. Dana still couldn't breathe, but it no longer really mattered as she felt her awareness fuzz up around the edges. Her luminous eyes started to glaze. She no longer could see peripherally, but if she concentrated very hard she could still see David well enough, and the anguish in his eyes. It was ripping him apart she could see, and she knew that he was feeling her pain along with her. She knew how hellish that could be. She'd experienced it before, knew how it crippled, how it hurt. She felt herself go even more fuzzy and she wondered what death would be like. She hoped it wouldn't hurt too badly. At that thought, she remembered, for some strange reason, the dream of the knifing and smiled painfully at the memory. 'You see,' she whispered soundlessly, lips moving with no air. Only he could hear her. Only he knew what she was saying. 'I couldn't save myself, either.' And out of pity for him and his tortured mind, she deliberately blocked off herself so that he wouldn't feel any more pain, and as the awareness of what she'd done shuddered through him, she fell into darkness.

CHAPTER TEN

SHE'D been in the darkness for so long and she felt so heavy, it was time to let go. It was time to leave this heavy body. Everything was too dark and painful, she she didn't want any more pain. And so Dana pushed out of her body and started to float away. The darkness was receding, and she no longer felt pain. There was light up ahead, a gentle, golden light that made the darkness and the pain a thing of the past. She went towards that with a feeling of joy.

But then she heard someone call her from behind, from the darkness, and she automatically jerked to a halt to listen. It was a strange sort of call, a whisper really, nothing more, but it held her as surely as if it had been a manacle of steel. She resisted, straining for the light, but then she recognised the voice of the one calling her.

He was in pain, too. She grew puzzled, for she dimly remembered stopping that pain. Then she realised that it was the pain of fear and grief, and it was all for her. He was whispering a name over and over again, and with a jolt she realised that it was what her name used to be. Through the desperation ran a thread of exhaustion and hopelessness. He thought she was leaving for good. She attempted to tell him that she was not really dying but merely going to another place, but she found that she could not get him to hear. So she looked, from the light to the darkness, back and forth, in an agony of indecision. It would be so easy to slide away into that warmth and light up ahead. It would be so very easy. But she knew who was calling her now, and she remembered that she had once loved him. His pain and his grief were unnecessary. She turned her back to the light and went back down into the darkness, reluctantly. After all, she told herself, there was always time later on to go back. Someday, she knew, she would go to the light. And the darkness consumed her until she knew neither the darkness nor the light, nor anything of the man who sat by her side in a lone vigil.

When Dana opened her eyes, she became aware of two things simultaneously. She was staring up at something white, and she was covered all over with cotton. No, that wasn't right, she thought, and she turned her head to look down at her body curiously. At least she thought she had turned her head to look at her body, but nothing had happened. She tried again and was astonished to find the simple movement of lifting her head incredibly hard. Sweat broke out on her forehead and her neck muscles strained before she was finally able to get her head off the pillow long enough to look down the length of her body.

Exhausted, she let her head fall back and pain lanced through it as she thought to herself, silly. There wasn't any cotton down there. There were some strange lumps, but absolutely no cotton.

And someone came through the door just outside of her range of vision. She turned her head slightly to the left, and that too was such an effort that she had to close her eyes to rest. She felt her hand taken and held carefully, and the warmth of another human's touch was such a pleasurable feeling, it made her smile. She opened her eyes and looked her love to her mother, who was bending over her with a tired, drawn face. When Denise saw her daughter look up and smile so sweetly, her eyes filled with tears, and she squeezed the hand that lay so limply in hers.

'I'm always ... such a burden to you,' Dana whispered, and watched a tear fall. Her mother shook her head gently. 'Jenny?'

Denise reached out and stroked her forehead with cool fingers. 'Yes, Jenny's fine. You pushed her out of the way in time.'

'Mick?'

'In jail for drunken driving and malicious conduct. Why are you asking about him? How are you feeling, darling? Are you in pain?'

Dana just smiled as she closed her eyes and the smile was one of compassion and sadness. 'Poor boy ...' she murmured, and slept.

Silence met her next awareness and she lay for some time with her eyes closed, drifting. Then she slid her hand over the top of the covers, feeling her fingers tremble from weakness, turning it over so that it lay with palm up, an invitation. A hand immediately closed over it, a large, calloused, masculine hand. David held hers as if it were something infinitely precious. A tear trembled at the corner of her eye and suddenly slipped away to soak into her hair. Another followed, and then another, for the cotton was no longer there, but the pain was and it jabbed throughout her whole body.

Something scraped, and David was stroking her

head while lifting the hand he held and cradling it against his chest. Lips shaking, she whispered, 'It would have been easier to go . . .'

'I know,' he whispered. 'But don't say it. You didn't go, and now you no longer have the choice.' A long, silent pause, and then, full of emotion, 'Dana? Did you really want to go so very badly?'

Such a wealth of sorrow, she thought, and forced her eyelids open to stare at him. He seemed different somehow, tired, worried. 'Not really,' she whispered, a mere thread of sound. Her eyes smiled at him for a moment and then closed. 'I was just—very tired . . . couldn't handle the pain by myself . . .' She stopped and gathered her strength so that she could whisper, 'I want to live.' Lips pressed against her forehead and again she slept.

A few days later, Dana was eating with help from one of the student nurses when her door opened and David again walked into the room. He'd visited every day, quite often for several hours at a time, reading to her, or talking and helping to pass away some of the time made tedious by pain and boredom. Dana carefully blanked out her mind, as she had for his past several visits, and she smiled at him lightly before taking a bite of vegetable.

He stood there and looked down at her silently for some time before finally saying, 'Hello.' She mumbled a greeting around her mouthful, wrinkled her nose at him, and turned her head back to the student nurse. Her heart was thudding at a mad pace and her hands shook like they hadn't for several days. David was waiting, just standing there quietly, and she knew he wasn't waiting for the student nurse to finish.

After an eternity, during which her appetitite had completely diminished, the nurse finally picked up her tray and left the room, and Dana was left alone with the silent, watching man who had perched himself on the wide hospital window sill. He was staring at her face, and she turned it away to look at the opposite wall.

'What's going on in that busy little mind of yours?' he asked conversationally, and she swallowed nervously. It didn't make the lump in her throat go away. 'You must know that I've felt your block for the past several days. What have you been thinking about, I wonder? Why do you close up like a tight little clam every time I get through that door?'

'No reason,' she whispered, clenching her hand into the top sheet until her knuckles whitened. 'No reason.'

'I don't even know why you bother to lie to me,' he said pleasantly. Her mouth shook. 'But I'll tell you this, Dana. You aren't going to get away with it. Sooner or later, I'm going to make you tell me what's making you do this.' He waited and then said softly, 'Look at me.'

'No.' She screwed her eyes tightly shut and kept her face turned resolutely away.

'Look at me, Dana!'

'No, I said!' Footsteps marched determinedly her way, and she felt a moment of intense frustration at her lack of mobility before hard fingers grasped at her chin and forced her head his way. She resisted but was too weak, and her face was taken firmly between his hands and cupped.

'Dana, I'm only going to say it one more time,' he told her gently. 'Look at me right this instant——'

'All right!' she shouted, and coughed at the pain in her ribs as she glared her helpless rage at him. He seemed very calm, as he let his eyes travel over her furious features. After just staring at him hatefully for a few moments, she said hardly, 'There, have you seen what you wanted to see? Are you satisfied now?'

'Yes,' he said strangely. 'I think I am.' He loosened his hold and just touched her face lightly, gently, his thumbs starting to stroke at the base of her jawline, on vulnerable skin. She quivered and shut her eyes again.

'Then get out.'

He continued as if she hadn't spoken. 'Do you want me to tell you what I saw?' She remained stubbornly silent, and he went on patiently. 'I saw a very frightened young girl just now. I wonder what has made her so afraid. Something has, in the past few days. What could it be?' He lifted one hand and smoothed the hair off Dana's forehead. She suddenly grabbed at both of his hands in order to try to push him away, but he captured her wrists and held her clenched fists against his chest as he positioned himself on the edge of the bed and leaned over her, too near. She gulped and shuddered, and tried desperately to get herself in control. She was too damned weak.

'Whatever it is, do you think you could just let go of it?' he asked her gently, pressing her hands into his shirt. She felt his pulse. 'It can't really matter in the long run, can it? Let's talk about something else. There's something I've been wanting very much to ask you.'

'No! Not now, all right?' she choked, renewing her efforts to get her hands free. His own tightened on hers so hard it hurt and she sucked in her breath, collapsing in defeat. 'Just go away and leave me alone, please.' It wasn't a request; it was a moan of anguish.

He sat very still, eyes sharp on her, expression stern. 'Whatever is hurting you so much is about me, isn't it?' he asked slowly. 'What have I done to upset you so, Dana? Whatever it is, I'm sorry for it. Why won't you talk to me?'

His gentleness was too much. She turned her face away and started to cry, and in her misery let her guard slip and her emotions spill through. He hissed, and with her guard down she felt a ripple of pure rage ripple through him. He grabbed at her chin and forced her head around again, his features hard and set. 'Who told you, dammit?' he gritted. 'Answer me! They weren't supposed to say anything yet!'

She lifted both her hands to her mouth as she sobbed. 'No one told me! I—I just knew, that's all. When the doctors came in to check on me a few days ago, I just knew! It—it's no one's fault. It just happened. Like the accident,' she said miserably.

He fought to get his shocked surprise under control, fought to control his expression. 'Then you know everything?' he asked quietly.

She said with great difficulty, 'I know that my spinal column was damaged pretty badly. I know that I most probably won't be able to walk again, if that's what you mean.'

He looked away, jaw muscle working. 'There's a chance you may walk again, Dana. Don't rule out that chance.'

'I don't.' She didn't look at him. 'But I've got to be realistic. I've got to prepared for any eventuality.'

He asked, 'Dana, please, will you marry me?'

She replied as quietly, with great finality, 'No.'

'I love you.' It was a simple, heartfelt statement, and a plea.

'And I love you.' In spite of her efforts, her words trembled in the air horribly.

'Then you can't say no.' He reached down, half turned on the bed, and brought his face down to hers. He didn't kiss her right away but instead looked clearly into her eyes, the honesty in his own, together with the strength of his emotion reaching into her very soul. His eyes were vulnerable, searching, loving. His face was harsh and yet gentle, the rough features softened, the dark hair falling on his brow. 'I love you, Dana. I love your smiles, and I love your warmth. I love your gentleness, your passionate sincerity, and your caring of others. I love your beautiful eyes, your lovely hair, your laughter, your sadness. I love your weaknesses and your strengths, and the femininity that is so inherently you. I love your faith and your gifts. Please don't block me out. Please don't send me away. You once said that you had the strength to stay, and that if I chose to go, I could. But now I'm the one who wants to stay, with you, and you are the one who wants to go.'

'I'm crippled,' she said clearly, in the clarity a wealth of fear and pain and helplessness was held.

'Don't say that! You're not crippled. You're the most whole person I've ever known. You may not be able to walk, but you are not crippled.'

'I won't marry you.'

'I won't accept that.'

'Leave me alone!' she screamed at him, feeling as if her heart would break, pushing away with both hands at his shoulders. He grabbed her hands and forced them down as he leaned his head into her shoulder and buried his face in her hair. He didn't try to fight with her, and he didn't try to reason with her. After her first shocked moment of stillness, she caught such a strong and overwhelming tidal wave of love and longing and hope from him that she was rocked to her core. She'd never known another person quite like him before in her life: he was such a powerful man, with such powerful feelings, and he could overwhelm her every time with himself.

She turned her head and buried her face against his, gave a great sob, and whispered, 'I'm not strong enough to handle this.'

'Hush. You're the strongest woman I know.' He began to kiss her all over her face.

'I'm not. I'm not.'

'I'll be your strength.'

'I'm so scared, I've never been so scared in my entire life,' she murmured in a moan, kissing him back, on his cheekbone, his jawline, the side of his nose, anywhere she could reach. 'I'm so scared it makes me sick to my stomach, I can't——'

'Oh, Dana, don't.' He drew back, looked down into her eyes, and smiled tenderly. 'You're so precious to me. I was never so horrified in my life as I was when I watched you tumble through the air like a rag doll, and I felt your pain and your shock, your disbelief that it was actually happening. When you nearly died, I'd thought I'd never seen anything more beautiful than when I saw you as a bright slim, ethereal figure, running freely towards a great, wonderful light, and my feet were bound to the ground so that I couldn't follow you. I saw your eagerness, and I called you back. You were in this hospital bed, and in reality you looked so small and white and still. The doctors had already told me that you might never walk again, and what I did was totally selfish. I didn't call you back for you, I called you back for me. And what I'm asking right now is totally selfish, for no other reason but that I want, and need it more than I've wanted or needed anything in my life. I love all of you, every single thing about you, and I'll beg. Don't leave me. You refused to ask anything of me, but I'm asking something of you now. Please don't leave me.'

There was no way she could put up the barrier again. He was in too deep, too strongly. She would never get him out of her heart or her life. She put out her arms and he came down to her, covering her mouth as his eyes closed in great, shuddering relief, and she surrendered her fears and uncertainties as she surrendered her mouth. And he absorbed it all, providing an immense well of strength and love for her to draw upon. She leaned on him.

CHAPTER ELEVEN

SHE sat, peacefully lounging under the wide, thick shade of the maple tree. A book lay on the dark green cushioning grass beside her. She drew her sweater around her slim shoulders, for the days were getting a bit chilly. The air was tranquil, bright light and mottled, shading leaves. Happiness was living inside of her, a constant healthy glow. She felt that her world was overflowing with the goodness and richness of life.

Across the beautifully cared for lawn, in the old, spacious home that was hers, the sound of the distant clicking of typewriter keys stopped and after a few moments a large, dark figure appeared in the doorway. The man searched with his eyes until he found her under the maple tree. He smiled, white teeth in a dark face, and walked over to sit down the grass beside her.

'How's the story coming?' she asked him lightly, reaching out and pushing back the lock of hair that had fallen over his brow.

He grinned at her. 'I think another five weeks or so should finish it. I'll be well ahead of the deadline.'

She was pleased. 'Good! And then we'll take that vacation you've been promising me for the last year.'

'Mmn,' he growled, and reached over to kiss her lingeringly. 'And we'll lie in the sun and make love on the beach . . .'

She murmured laughingly, eyes half closed, 'Won-

derful love . . . whoever would have thought that our
mental sensitivity to one another could make it so
delicious?' His eyes laughed at her as he kissed her
again.

'. . . and I'll be thinking of the sequel for the
book——'

'. . . and I will beat you if you do!' she exclaimed
indignantly. He laughed again and picked up the book
that lay on the grass beside her, opening it curiously
and then cocking a quizzical eyebrow at her.

'You've been out here for a good hour with that
book open,' he accused. 'I saw you when I came down
for coffee, and you haven't turned a page yet! You're
right where you were last night. What've you been
doing out here, anyway?'

She looked away, to the house, and felt his
unspoken concern. 'I've been looking back.'

His voice was very quiet. 'Good thoughts?'

'Oh, yes!' Her response was immediate and total,
and she felt his relief. A welling of tenderness rose up
inside of her at that. He still could be unsure. 'I've
been thinking of all that you've given me. You've
made me so very happy. We have a good life here,
David. But when I look back, I get such a strange
feeling when I think of how we met and what we went
through together. Peter still calls it our "mutual need",
but though I can see what you helped me with, I can't
really understand what I did for you. If I hadn't
experienced the flashback, you would have, sooner or
later, and you would have got help.'

'Would I have?' he asked strangely. She faltered and
looked at him uncertainly as he stared at a chittering
bird in the tree. 'Or wasn't I more along the path of no

return? As I recall, I was breaking myself with my rigidity. No, my love, the one essential thing that you gave to me and that you still give me every night with your sweet, warm body and your eager loving, and every day with your peaceful tranquillity—the one thing that I drink from you constantly and always come away refreshed—is,' he turned his head and looked into her eyes, 'redemption.' They stared at each other for a long moment, and it was a silent giving and taking, a mutual sharing and a mutual filling. The wind blew through the tree leaves above, and a few fell to the ground in a scattered, random pattern. Then he smiled at her, and the smile was a communication of continued love and affection and human desire. 'Come, sweetheart. It's time to go inside.'

And after he stood, he bent to pick up her slight form and deposit her in the chair that waited nearby, wheeling her into the house.

 **ROMANCE**

Next month's romances from Mills & Boon

Each month, you can choose from a world of variety in romance with Mills & Boon. These are the new titles to look out for next month.

FOR ADULTS ONLY Charlotte Lamb
FLIGHT TO PASSION Flora Kidd
DOLPHINS FOR LUCK Peggy Nicholson
NO HOLDS BARRED Jessica Steele
A CHANGE OF HEART Sandra Field
THE DEVIL'S PAWN Yvonne Whittal
ONE LAST DANCE Claire Harrison
TROPICAL EDEN Kerry Allyne
HEIDELBERG WEDDING Betty Neels
LOVERS' KNOT Marjorie Lewty
RAGE Amanda Carpenter
BRIDE BY CONTRACT Margaret Rome

Buy them from your usual paperback stockist, or write to: Mills & Boon Reader Service, P.O. Box 236, Thornton Rd, Croydon, Surrey CR9 3RU, England. Readers in South Africa-write to: Mills & Boon Reader Service of Southern Africa, Private Bag X3010, Randburg, 2125.

Mills & Boon
the rose of romance

Take 4 Exciting Books Absolutely FREE

Love, romance, intrigue... all are captured for you by Mills & Boon's top-selling authors. By becoming a regular reader of Mills & Boon's Romances you can enjoy 6 superb new titles every month plus a whole range of special benefits: your very own personal membership card, a free monthly newsletter packed with recipes, competitions, exclusive book offers and a monthly guide to the stars, plus extra bargain offers and big cash savings.

AND an Introductory FREE GIFT for YOU.
Turn over the page for details.

As a special introduction we will send you four exciting Mills & Boon Romances Free and without obligation when you complete and return this coupon.

At the same time we will reserve a subscription to Mills & Boon Reader Service for you. Every month, you will receive 6 of the very latest novels by leading Romantic Fiction authors, delivered direct to your door. You don't pay extra for delivery — postage and packing is always completely Free. There is no obligation or commitment — you can cancel your subscription at any time.

You have nothing to lose and a whole world of romance to gain.

Just fill in and post the coupon today to MILLS & BOON READER SERVICE, FREEPOST, P.O. BOX 236, CROYDON, SURREY CR9 9EL.

Please Note:- READERS IN SOUTH AFRICA write to Mills & Boon, Postbag X3010, Randburg 2125, S. Africa.

FREE BOOKS CERTIFICATE

To: Mills & Boon Reader Service, FREEPOST, P.O. Box 236, Croydon, Surrey CR9 9EL.

Please send me, free and without obligation, four Mills & Boon Romances, and reserve a Reader Service Subscription for me. If I decide to subscribe I shall, from the beginning of the month following my free parcel of books, receive six new books each month for £6.60, post and packing free. If I decide not to subscribe, I shall write to you within 10 days. The free books are mine to keep in any case. I understand that I may cancel my subscription at any time simply by writing to you. I am over 18 years of age.

Please write in BLOCK CAPITALS.

Signature _____

Name _____

Address _____

_____ Post code _____

SEND NO MONEY — TAKE NO RISKS.

Please don't forget to include your Postcode.

Remember, postcodes speed delivery. Offer applies in UK only and is not valid to present subscribers. Mills & Boon reserve the right to exercise discretion in granting membership. If price changes are necessary you will be notified.

6R   Offer expires June 30th 1985

EP86